THE STAGES

The Stages
Gabrysia Rocha

This is a work of fiction. Any resemblance to locations or persons, living or dead, is entirely coincidental. Names, characters, events and places are either the product of the author's imagination or used fictitiously.

Copyright © 2022 by Gabrysia Rocha

All rights reserved. No part of this book may be reproduced in any form by an electronic or mechanical means, including informational storage and retrieval systems, without permission in writing from the author, except by a reviewer, who may quote brief passages in an interview.

ISBN 979-8-3626-4310-2 (paperback)

"Grief is merely a stage, with an audience of your peers to watch you fall apart."

Table of Contents.

Prologue	1
Stage I – Shock	3
Stage II – Denial	9
Interlude I – A Time long forgotten	18
Stage III – Guilt	23
Stage IV – Anger	30
Interlude II – Old Habits die Hard	37
Stage V – Bargaining	41
Stage VI – Distress	37
Interlude III – A Brief Moment of Realisation	52
Stage VII – Depression	56
Stage VIII – Loneliness	61
Interlude IV – A Divergence in Life	66
Stage IX – Acceptance	134

Prologue.

"She was like any normal girl. Studious, focused, respectable. And then it happened."

Early morning.

Heaven knows how long she was studying her textbooks intently last night. The fact that she slept so late and woke so early hadn't done wonders for her, only causing her painful exhaustion to amplify as she swayed to and fro after standing from the chair in front of her desk. A long night to precede a long day. That's how life went for Violet LaFramboise, but she wouldn't trade it for the world. She loved it – her life's work had led up to this, and she was proud of where she had gotten. The onslaught of tiredness that came with it definitely didn't do her any favours, though.

Stepping down the stairs cautiously in her rather tired state, she stumbled for a moment. Hung from the banister in panic, she swiped for the rail again. Tumbling down the stairs, her hand had slipped. Crash! There she was, sprawled out on the floor with an aching head – not only from the way she had careened headfirst from the top of the stairs – diving out of the way to avoid the falling shelf above her. Heaving breaths filled the silence. Kneeling up, she placed a hand over her heart. Christ, that was close.

Clearing up the mess she had caused with her own clumsiness, she quickly reached for a screwdriver she kept on another shelf for this exact scenario (since it, as she had moments prior, was prone to tumbling down dramatically) and fixed the fallen object to the wall once more. Tightening the screw until her hand ached and cramped relentlessly, she was almost certain it wouldn't – no, *couldn't* – fall again. Almost certain.

Finally making her way into the kitchen, she poured herself a cup of tea and placed it on the table as the rustling of papers caught her attention. Walking over to her door, she had just caught a glimpse of the letter flap shutting, the sonorous clang filling up the space around her as she crouched down at the letter on the floor. Picking up the blank, sealed envelope, naught but her address scrawled into the paper, she headed back into the kitchen and sat at the table, sipping on her tea with one hand and using her other carefully to open the letter.

… Oh.

Well, that's strange, she thought to herself quietly, *it's unlike him to contact me.* It was indeed unlike him; he had, time and time again, stated he wanted nothing to do with her after 'the shit she puts him through', and yet here, he had written the infamous letter. Folding the paper back up, the rustling of her slotting it into the envelope once again became synonymous with the blisteringly cold wind outside, battering on her windows relentlessly as she gently closed the letter again.

Now all she had to do was await his arrival.

Stage I.

Shock

"She couldn't believe her ears when she heard it. She didn't believe it. She didn't have it in her to."

"Michael."

"Violet."

The stare they shared in that moment was cold. Unfeeling. Hers was clearly filled with more surprise than rage, and his was encompassed by an unshakeable sense of entitlement.

"I'm not giving you anything." She answered to him with a calm tone, ready to wave him off and shut him out, but he was intent on staying. Barging past her to enter her abode, the slam of the door, caused by the astringent, relentless wind, was enough to knock the slightly loosened shelf from her wall again. She winced at the crash, but waved it off to follow her brother, deciding to fix it later.

"How do you know I want something?" Michael told her sharply, folding his arms in a combative manner.

"You *always* want something, Michael. Your sense of desire is practically innate."

"I liked it better when you refused to talk."

"Invent time travel. Then, you can return to that." Drawing her hands over the tablecloth she had laid previously on her kitchen table, Violet dusted off the crumbs of whatever she had eaten last and settled in her normal seat, awaiting her brother to do the same. Crossing his arms tighter, Michael noticed Violet mirroring his actions and did the same, seating himself at the table too, gripping an apple within his hand and taking a bite as Violet continuously lectured him.

"How much are you going to drop to your knees and plead for this time? One thousand? Three? Perhaps the whole world will satisfy you." She raised her nose at him after she had finished speaking with a disdain surrounding her, certainly displeased at his presence. "After all, you live to hold people back."

"How are you so certain that I want something?"

"I've already answered that question."

Michael bit down on his apple again and chewed. It bought him time to think about what to respond with. Violet was difficult, true, but he was determined to get through to her. He wouldn't have been there if it wasn't important, anyway. However, importance was particularly subjective when it came to the pair of them. "Maybe I *want* to tell you something."

"Tell me anything." Violet shrugged nonchalantly at that, standing to move toward her kettle, picking it from its stand to take a step to the right and fill it with water. "Nothing will convince me to give you anything more than I already have."

Huffing at her stubborn nature, Michael sank his teeth into his apple again. She wouldn't budge. This time, he was right; he really *didn't* want anything from her, though. He only wanted to tell her something. It almost felt as if she knew, and was trying to avoid the topic altogether, but he was almost certain she was clueless. He had a good inkling of what she would be like if she wasn't.

"You look like a mess," he began, shrugging to himself. He felt it necessary to voice his opinions, seeing as she was shutting him down so easily. He needed the little win, that sense of being above her that he always used to have. Obviously, it was long gone – but, perhaps for the sake of nostalgia or maybe his own failed life, he still took the dig at her regardless. "Reminds me of when we were kids."

"I don't care. That time is long gone. Like I said, go and invent time travel, if you want to see me like that so badly." She answered him distinctly, glare tightening. She had a tough grip around him and knew exactly how he liked to play his cards. She was always better at chess, anyway, though dabbled in the art of beating him at every game he tried to play with her.

"So, nothing's changed?"

"For you, apparently. You still want the world from me."

"Better to ask than take, eh?"

"Michael, just get lost if you're going to behave petulantly." She rolled her eyes at his colloquial language, holding her head in her hand as she sipped on the tea she had just about brewed for herself. Barely seven minutes, and she was already bored to death of his antics. "I don't have time for your nonsense."

"Penelope."

The singular name was enough to snap Violet out of her irritation. "What about them?" Violet knew almost instantly who he was talking about – a childhood friend, of course, one she valued dearly. "I'm surprised you even recall them. It seems most of your childhood was spent ruining mine." At that, she couldn't help but laugh softly at her own self-deprecating retort, laced in sarcasm and bitter disappointment, sitting in her seat again with her hot cup of tea, freshly made and resting in her palms to warm the fragile fingers extending from it.

Noticing how Michael's expression saddened slightly, she felt a minimal amount of worry prick at her fragile heart. Why was he mentioning Penelope? He had nothing to do with them. What business did he have, bringing their name up? "What's that expression for?" She prodded at him, a slight aggression in her tone. The pricking feeling had turned from a stabbing to a carving. Now she was becoming desperate. "Speak to me, damn it."

"They're–..."

"They're *what?!*" Slamming her curled fists on the table, she felt herself tremble, the panic coursing through her body. Violet reserved herself at that, moving back into her seat. She didn't have the time, nor the energy, to fight him. She had wasted all of it on getting to where she was now with him. There was no point in battling him for anything. Keep calm.

"They... God, can you *not* look at me like that?! At this point, it's better off you don't know." Michael stood to take his leave, hoisting his satchel over his shoulder until he felt a hand grip onto his parka-jacket sleeve.

"Michael," Violet was now laughing slightly, though her hands were shaking. His eyebrows furrowed and raised in accordance with his shock, sitting in his seat again as the woman before him took in a sharp breath. "*Please.* Tell me what happened to them." Watching as she took her seat again, he felt the guilt whittle away at his heart as he went quiet for the next moment. Her attachment to Penny was unparalleled – there truly was nothing like the pair of them together.

"So?" Violet questioned, calm once more.

"So *what?*" Michael retorted, trying to act foolish to avoid telling her.

"What happened to them?" Of course, it wouldn't work.

Taking in a deep breath, he placed his palms together, each of his fingers curling around the back of his hands as he tried to formulate a response. He never once imagined himself having to tell her this, yet, here he was, trying his damn best to break the news to her. He couldn't do it, but he had to.

"They're… gone."

"Gone? Gone where?" Violet started again, standing to her weakening feet as she pressed her own palms to the tablecloth. Her fingernails sank into the fabric, leaving little imprints on the cream cloth as she stared at him like a deer in headlights. She had so much to say, yet no way to articulate herself. "What the Hell is 'gone' supposed to mean–?"

"They're just… *gone.* To Heaven, if you will."

The silence inside the house deafened everything else. Not even the beating of the cold, unruly wind outside on the windows, or the sound of the gentle hail chipping away at the glass, or the whistling seeping in through the chimney-hole could top how dead-silent the house had fallen.

"You're… not being serious, are you?" Violet's choked-up voice broke the near-impenetrable quiet.

"Would I lie to you?" Michael's own tone had become uncharacteristically sympathetic to Violet's situation, standing also, only to shuffle his chair over beside her and seat himself down once more.

"Of course, you would. That's all you ever do."

"That isn't true."

"Of course, it is!" Raising her voice, she stared at him with a rather indecipherable expression. Not quite angry, sorrowful, grief-stricken or blank. It was definitely something– contorted to the point where she almost looked ugly but pertaining to a sort of inability to pinpoint what exactly she was feeling. "Of course, you would pull some shit like this to weasel money, or- or a place to stay out of me. That– that is *unbelievably* characteristic of you, using Penny's death to do something like that!"

Sighing as he stood up, he gripped his bag in his hand again and handed her a second letter. She opened it with a frantic breath in, forcing her nails underneath the envelope to tear it open and shove her hand into the gap created. Scanning her eyes over the paper as it unfolded, she bit down on her lip as tiny droplets fell from her eyes, sinking into the ruffled tablecloth. "It's not true," she sighed breathily, "it- it's just not true." Repeating the affirmation to herself, she threw the letter to Michael again, stumbling backwards.

"Violet, *please*," he started, though was quickly met with her panic in both a metaphorical and physical manner. Stumbling backwards from the slap he had sustained from her; he was about to challenge her actions until he saw her. Pupils dilated, a myriad of bodily fluids running down her flushed cheeks. She was near unrecognizable, in a state like that.

"What is wrong with you?! Why would you show me this? Why would you tell me any of this?" She sobbed out, holding onto his clothing as her knees began to buckle. Staring up at him, her face became drenched with tears again as she wailed, her knees as weak as her heart. "Are you doing this because you want to hurt me?" The words stumbled out of her mouth like lost hikers on a mountain. "Do you like to see me suffer?"

Stumbling back from her iron grip, he tried to pull her hands away by the wrists but was only met with her holding on tighter. "I'm doing this because you deserve to know!" He shouted back, unintentionally mimicking her rage-filled tone as he finally got her to unclench her fingers from his jacket. Watching as she stumbled and then fell to her knees, he couldn't ignore the twinge of guilt flashing through his mind like a lightning bolt.

"... Do you really hate me that much?" Sobbing out the sentence, Violet stared at him with rather saddened eyes. Two glossy, round, near perfect spheres of pure anguish and brokenness.

"I don't hate you–"

"Yes, you do. You hate me." Violet cut him off sharply. "I know you hate me… I know *why* you hate me."

"Tell me." He folded his arms, now slightly curious to her reasoning. "Why do I hate you, then?"

"You want things from me… things that I won't give you."

Then came the silence again. It hurt them both for different reasons. Violet's mind was blank as ever – Michael's was racing wildly. Neither of them could think of anything to fill the silence, except for Violet's silent sobs and the hail outside, banging down on the window like millions upon millions of tiny fists, punching at the glass to get in.

"What do you want from me?"

"I don't want *anything*. All I really wanted was to tell you… *that.*" Michael raised his hands to his chest defensively, stepping back as his palms began sweating. The idea of him being a bad person was so ingrained into Violet's mind that she couldn't even believe her best friend had died without jumping to the conclusion that it was all a plot for him to get something out of her. On some level, he felt bad about what he had done to her, but still didn't know what to do about it. In his eyes, the damage had already been done – there was nothing he could do about her hurt now. Even now, he was still lying to her – he really *did* want money from her, but obviously didn't have the heart to tell her now. Not in an all-too-familiar state like that.

"I already told you, damn it. You *always* want something." She answered, sitting down on her cold, hard, linoleum floor with her legs curled up to her chest, facing the door to lean her head on her knees and look up at him with that same, imperceptible expression. "You… you wouldn't tell me this if you didn't want to get something out of me." The spite filling her tone was now more palpable, seeing as she was still wholly convinced that he was lying. It was all he ever did. Rather, it was all he knew how to do.

Sighing as he gripped his bag tighter for the last time, he tossed the letter he had been holding for the past few minutes onto the table and began to wander toward the general direction of the door.

"Where are you going?" She asked, scrambling to her feet as her legs began to carry her closer to her brother. It didn't even feel like she could think for herself. All she could do was speak. Babble on about God knows what, and maybe she would get somewhere.

"Home. Where else am I supposed to go? You don't want me here, and you've made it clear you don't want to listen to reason."

"Michael!" She screamed his name, viscerally, the volume and growl in her voice tearing away at her vocal cords. "Michael, don't go! Please! Don't go, don't leave me! Don't leave!" She called out to him, swiping at his coat as he pulled it out of her reach. Running to the door, Michael's heavy breaths went in tandem with his and Violet's footsteps, trying to escape her as he raced her to his car.

"Get away from me! You wanna treat me like shit?! You want me gone?!" Quickly running into his car, he slammed the door and yelled over the protection of the glass windows that Violet was banging on, fighting with the muffling aspect of it to get his message across. "Fine, then! I'll go!"

As he drove away, she felt her heart crack a little. This wasn't happening to her. She wasn't *alone* alone, was she? Before, it was just normal alone. Before, she still had the opportunity to stop being lonely. She had the chance to reach out and tell somebody she felt lonely, and perhaps go out and do something with them. She had people there for her. She just chose to live her life in solitude.

Now, she was *alone* alone. Now, she didn't have that opportunity to tell somebody she was lonely. She was simply lonely. Now, there was nothing she could do about being alone. Nothing to mend, nothing to break.

As she sank her knees into the snow beneath her feet, her pained screams echoing through the desolate, blanketed forest, she came to the bitter realisation that she was *alone.*

Stage II.

Denial

"'It's fine.' That's what she said over and over again, wasn't it? 'I'm fine,' 'everything's fine,' just so she would convince herself that it was."

"How did they die?"

"What?"

"I'm asking you a question, Michael. Answer me." The pain in her voice became more and more evident as she continued to pester him for answers. Holding onto her telephone tightly, the wire curled around Violet's fragile fingers began to constrict around her hand, her fingertips falling as cold as her heart. "Please. I just need to know how they died."

A sigh came over the telephone. "If I tell you, you'll only spiral more." His answer only led to more questions as she pressed her palm to the desk she was sat at, sending an array of papers fluttering through the cold, winter air surrounding her. She hadn't put the heating on – she hadn't found the resolve or energy to. "Just go, and… mourn their death, or whatever."

"Michael!" She screamed over the phone, her grip tightening. By now, her hand was near falling off her wrist from the way the cord had tied itself around her arm. "Don't fucking toy with me! Tell me how they died!"

Sure, Michael had seen her at her worst. Or, rather, what he perceived as her worst. Dishevelled hair, poor health, obsession with grades, never speaking to anyone. "I'm not telling you, when you're in a state like this!" He barked over the phone with the same anger she displayed. However, over the phone, he was settled in his dirtied room with a glass of beer beside him, just about as shocked as he could get. He had never heard her swear at him like that. Sure, occasionally, when he stopped by to ask for a little bit of extra cash to pay off his debts, or maybe a place to stay for the next few nights, she would tell him to 'get lost if he's going to pull this shit' in a tired, disappointed voice, but this was different.

This was unbridled grief. She had reached her breaking point. He had failed to push her to it himself, all those years ago, when he still held the power to do so, but now all he could do was sit in the side-lines and watch her fall apart. He nearly, just nearly, pitied her for it; once a respectable woman in her field, a doctor, at that, reduced to nothing but a grief-stricken, broken individual.

"Michael, I'm going to ask you nicely again." She broke the impenetrable silence with a slightly whispering tone, standing to her feet to try and ground herself properly, leaning on her desk and staring at the falling snow outside. The next day had brought on a softer attitude to the weather, though she knew it could just as easily take a turn for the worse. "Tell me how they died, or I'm going to come and find you and *make you*."

Taking a sharp breath in, the quiet that descended in Michael's room as his sister waited for a response. He didn't know what to say to her, at that point. "I already told you. I'm not going to tell you when you're acting like this." He spoke calmly, trying to keep his tone level and cool to not agitate her further. The last thing she needed from him was attitude, or disrespect, or something along those lines.

"I am *fine*."

"No, you are *not* fine."

"Yes I am!" It was like her mind was facing some sort of internal death. She couldn't even process that she was upset, but she still had the fight in her to argue with her brother. "Damn it, just tell me what happened to them! What is wrong with you?! Can't you do this much for me, after ruining everything else?!"

That was quick to strike Michael, forcing him to pull the phone away from his head. Was that really how she saw him? Just as somebody who had ruined her and tortured her? For a split-second, he impulsively felt proud of himself. He took up so much space in her mind that she devoted at least *some* amount of time to deciding she hated him. Regardless, he picked the phone from his desk again and began to shout back at her with the same barking tone she had used for him. "I didn't 'ruin everything else'! If it wasn't for me, you wouldn't have even fucking known this had happened!"

"You think I wouldn't have found out?!" Violet was back to screaming again. "You think that I wouldn't know when the one person who actually gave a shit about me *died?!* Are you *crazy?*" For a moment, she calmed herself, sitting at her desk again with her phone held loosely in her hand. A sudden light-headedness came over her, leaning her forehead into her free hand whilst she listened to his soft breaths through the phone. "You are *killing me* by withholding this information."

"Stop being dramatic."

"Fuck off." She didn't even have the energy to feel remorseful for what she had said. She wasn't going to let him talk down to her as if her best friend hadn't just died. She was too young. *Too soon,* she thought, *too soon, Penny. How could you leave me like this?* "I'm fine. I'm not being dramatic. Just tell me what happened to them."

"I'm not telling you."

"Yes, you are! You're going to fucking tell me what happened to them, or I swear to God, Michael—!"

Before she could tear him down more, he had severed the line, no longer entertaining her fit of rage. "Michael?" She asked into the high-pitched droning of the phone, trying to dial his number again. No response. "Michael! Michael, you *fucker!* Call me back!" She yelled out into the emptiness of her unkempt room, eventually allowing her anger to peel away and melt into an inescapable sadness.

Resting her head on her desk in tears, all she could do was cry. Sob, wail, punch the desk, whatever it took to get her emotions out. If she didn't broadcast it to anybody else, it was fine. She was fine. At the least, to everyone else, she would look fine. Taking in a deep breath, she heaved herself up from the desk and began to walk downstairs, leaving her room to plod down the staircase and move away from the fallen shelf, avoiding the books littering the floor in front of the stairs to sit in the kitchen and think.

All she could do was think, and yet, somehow, nothing came to mind. Violet's mind felt heavy, and empty; racing, and still; black, and white. There was nothing, and there was everything. Silently, she walked to the kettle, picking it up to fill it with water and boil it. Watching the bubbles slowly grow and rise to the top of the water seemed to pacify her for a moment, and she gained the strength to head to her living room and stare at the aquarium. In it, she felt herself melt away, watching the various fish swim about in the clear water. She could be at peace for the few seconds she needed to regain herself.

As she heard the kettle whistling away, almost too cheerfully, she wandered back over to the kitchen to pour the boiled water into a mug, then tossing in a teabag carelessly and taking it over to the table in the centre of the room. It had retained its previous state from last night, crumpled up and folded in the places that she had clawed at it in desperation, stained with small puddles of tears, sweat and saliva. Shuffling it away, so that she didn't have to be reminded of the inescapable events of last night, she threw the teabag in the direction of the small dish by the sink, missing horribly and watching powerlessly as it landed on the washing rack, dirtying a few of her nicely cleaned dishes from a few nights prior. She had simply forgotten to put them away.

Sipping on her tea quietly, she took a moment to pause and stare out of the window. It all seemed grey, now. Before, she could easily pick out the green of the pine trees and how much she loved the colour, or the purity in the white blanket of snow and how winter always held a special place in her heart, but now it was bland. Now all she could see was an endless sea of pine needles littering the area, stretching on as far as the eye could see, plaguing her home with the stench of the woods, or the aggression in the cold that forced her to turn the heating on and waste more of her money.

All Violet could ponder now was how. Was it gruesome? Brutal? Unjust? The multitude of questions only prodded at her conscience further. Why wouldn't Michael tell her? What was so bad about it that he had to hold back on her? What could have been elicited from her if she knew? Holding her head in her hands, she grabbed her teacup and threw it on the floor, watching as the fine porcelain scattered in all directions, her chest heaving up and down as she yelled. "It's not fair!" She was screaming to nobody in particular; with no-one there to listen, it was near impossible to tell who she was trying to communicate with.

"Damn him, damn them, damn it all!" Swiping the vase on her table from its rightful place, it too fell victim to her inconsolable rage as she helplessly saw it fall to her tiled floor and break into a million pieces. Crushing it all beneath her foot, she cared not for the glass digging past her sock to the sole of her foot, nor for the hot tea swirling in cold water now soaking the aforementioned fabric. "Why won't he tell me anything?! Why is he doing this to me?!" Screeching out her worries, she ran back upstairs with a wet sock, a bleeding foot, tangled auburn hair and tears streaming down her face.

Gripping her phone in her hands, she hurriedly dialled the number, the ringing of the dial in the centre of her phone melding with her shaky breaths. Waiting for someone, anyone, to pick up, she didn't care – she couldn't be alone. Not right now.

"Hello? Ludwig Residence?"

"Friedrich! I– I need to speak to Friedrich Ludwig, please," she choked out, patting her chest to attempt to soothe its incessant need for oxygen, "please, put Dr. Ludwig on the phone... *please...*"

There was silence for a moment. Tense silence. So thick and cold that Violet felt like she had been frozen in a block of ice, still and unmoving in the time that it had taken the other line to retrieve the person she was begging for.

"Hello? Who is it?"

"Dr. Ludwig? Is that you?" She sobbed out, praying to whatever God was torturing her with the sick game it was playing above her head, like a carrot being dangled just within reach to be yanked away and keep her on that edge of desperation, that he would answer with a yes.

"Violet?" Friedrich now sounded more frantic, yet still characteristically calm, as if he was hurrying around the room for something. He had always found it effortless to remain calm in a situation of mayhem. "Are you okay? You sound panicked. I'll come to visit you later. Stay put, okay?" Then the line cut off, and Violet slowly put down the phone.

He was coming over? Now? When? How long did she have to compose herself? Standing to her feet and beginning to pace, her mind had blanked almost as soon as her thoughts had begun racing, like they had just sped past her without a care in the world. At the least, there would be somebody she could confide in with her feelings. At the most, she would have a friend by her side to guide her while her shattered conscience clearly couldn't.

Trying to tidy herself up in the mirror, she continued to pick out little details that made her seem more upset and careless about herself. It had only been one day, and she already looked damaged enough – sunken eyes, bags discoloured with a deep black, paling skin, bitten nails. All of it made her look utterly destroyed. Trying to fix as much of it as she could, she settled on her bed and eventually curled up on top of the sheets in anticipation for Friedrich's arrival.

Staring at her wall, she felt struck by everything that had happened. It had hit her like a metal rod would have pierced her beating heart, leaving her to fall to the floor and bleed out with nobody to press their hands to the wound and say 'it will be okay', even if her chances of life were low as ever. Her eyes darted from crack to crack, from uneven dribbles of paint to tiny specks of random stains along the wall, trying to distract herself from everything going on in her mind.

After an extensive moment of fixating her vision on the imperfections in the wall, she fell to the grace of slumber, leaning into its calming, distracting embrace as she finally fell asleep.

*

Waking up to the harsh knocks on her door, Violet's eyes fluttered open, as if to combat the idea that they were going to close again and stay shut forever. Nonetheless, she forced herself up from her slumped position, swiping around on her bedside cabinet for her glasses and situating them on the bridge of her nose, with no care for how they slanted askew to her pupils, taking a glance at herself in the mirror with an almost palpable disdain, then carrying herself to the door. The grace and elegance that surrounded her had dissipated out for favour of a mental fog, perhaps clouding her judgement enough to reduce her to the shell of a woman she represented now.

Her face had fallen blank as she moved towards the door; not to say her face had a certain incapability to display emotion, but that the contorted nature of her features conveyed it all at once, in the manner that her true feelings became indecipherable. She couldn't even unhinge her maw to express shock, or perhaps widen her eyes in the similar emotion, or even crack a smile of sardonic glee. She just stared, maybe in disbelief or something along those lines.

"What are you doing here?" The words left her lips loosely, her hands subconsciously stuffed into her pockets, rummaging around and grazing the individual fingertips over each coin, paperclip and receipt buried within the fabric unceremoniously.

"Your friend, Dr. Friedrich Ludwig." The way the male of the pair had called out that name sent her mind running back to the moment she was trying oh-so-desperately, fighting tooth and nail, to forget, her hands clenching around a few cents as her entire body recoiled at the name. She didn't have anything against him – nor with Penny – but thinking, even for one second, that some star-crossed fate had befallen him caused a horrid shiver to overcome her. "He told us everything."

"Everything?" She finally lifted her head from the daze she was trapped in; the heat clung to her, gripping on each individual cell that made up her skin, sticking to her, and almost trapping her within that daze. She parted her chapped, reddening lips to speak again, but held her tongue and sank a little, half in shame and half in fear. "How much is 'everything'?"

"Yve, honey," the lady beside the first man started, reaching forward to place a hand on her shoulder – to which, again, she flinched and stumbled backwards – with a solemn look smothered on her face. If Violet knew any better, she wouldn't have looked up, for fear of the tears welled in her mother's eyes, but she had the sense to make momentary eye contact with her father, catching a glimpse of her distraught mother in the process. Perhaps she *didn't* know any better. "You're suffering…"

"I am *fine*," she reiterated, her heart thumping in her cold chest as the warmth around her continued to scratch away at her sanity, "and, frankly, I don't know why Friedrich sent you both to further my *torment*."

"*Torment?* Oh, listen here, young lady. We will *not* be taking any disrespect from the likes of *you*—" Her father began, but her mother was quicker to shut him down with an ice-cold, piercing glare.

"Don't you start that now, Vincent." The fragile woman hissed at him, fingers sinking into Violet's shoulder as she spoke before they loosened to gently caress Violet's shoulder. "Honey.. We can see it in you. You're suffering, Violet. Please, open up to us—"

"You don't get it." Her eyes travelled up, down and all around, nitpicking every little aspect of their presentation in the futile, desperate hopes to berate them. A tie too short on her father, an ill-fitting item of clothing on her mother, a pair of glasses slanted on either of their faces, even an untucked article of clothing would have satisfied her, but no. Every single thing, every tiny little detail of Violet's parents was perfect. An utter, inarguable depiction of perfection, and every second she spent, focused on the perfectly slicked hairs, or the perfectly ironed clothing, or the perfectly matched jewellery made her feel more inferior than she ever had in her entire life. "You will *never* get it."

"Yve, please, talk to us," her mother started again, but was quickly interrupted by her father.

"Do you seriously think we don't get it? You think me and your mother don't get it?" He began to step forward into her home, ignoring how she recoiled again and stumbled back, her eyebrows turning upwards, a clear expression of fear and anguish slathered on her face as he continually belittled her. "Me and your mother broke our backs out to make a living for you and your brother! How *dare* you disrespect our family name like that—!"

"My brother is a deadbeat narc who begs for money on his hands and knees because he's too damn lazy to get off his Davenport and make a life for himself!" Violet retorted back, her nose lifted in a sudden aggression. He could say what he liked about her, but as soon as she was put on the same pedestal as her brother, she drew the line. "Do *not* group me in with that failure of a man! He is *nothing* compared to me!" Taking in a deep breath as her sternum vibrated, the trembling in her sigh rattling it again, she turned her eyes to her fearful, solemn mother before turning her sights back to the enraged father standing in front of her.

"What? So, you think you're *so* much better than us – may I remind you, *all* of us," her father gestured towards her mother loosely, who looked as if she wanted to completely detach herself from the argument entirely, "just because you got multiple degrees in some prestigious college that, reminding you again, *we* let you go to at *sixteen*?!" Folding his arms with an unimpressed glare, Violet couldn't help but pause to formulate her response as her eyes travelled along his attire. The tie he wore was fastened beneath his paper-white collar in such a way that learning how to tie it would take longer than tying the fabric itself; after all, there was not a doubt in Violet's mind that he would ever reach a dishevelled state like hers.

"The difference between me and Michael is that *he* thinks he's better than us. I *know* I'm better than him. And, dare I say, I'm better than you, too." She folded her arms arrantly, watching how unceremoniously her father's frown deepened. It almost felt good to get a rise out of him. It made her feel something. Maybe a sense of pride, or perhaps fear – something telling her to run away, yet simultaneously to provoke him more. "I'm stronger than you, after all. I don't have to resort to childish insults and flippant behaviour to get my point a–"

Before she could retort to him more, she felt herself nearly hit the wall from the impact her father had placed upon her cheek. Her body slammed down onto the wall, slumping hurriedly to the floor as Violet clutched her bruising cheek, a galaxy of blues, purples and reds rising to the surface of her skin. "Vincent!" Her mother finally chimed in as the voice of reason, the aggressive clack of her heels filling up the ambient silence as she continually chastised him. "What is *wrong* with you? Are you crazy?! How could you hit your own daughter like that?!"

In the moments that she was curled on the floor, writhing on the planks of wood like some pathetic animal, an acme attacked by its predator, she felt her eyes close as she hit her head to the wall again. She couldn't hear anything happening around her for the most part, as her mother's chiding was quick to fade; just the consistent beat of her heart and the ringing sustained from the fall she had taken. Sure, her father was a burly, muscular and certainly masculine man, with the strength to prove it, but he hadn't hit her with nearly his full force. His full force could shatter a man's bones in a fraction of a second – to him, and her, this was a warning tap.

She would get what she deserved if she continued the way she had.

Staring up at the ceiling with bleary eyes, coated in thick globs of tears to trail down her face, blood to leak out of her nose and saliva to curl from her lips down her chin, she felt pathetic. *I'm fine, mother,* she wanted to mumble out, but couldn't even muster up the resolve inside of her to do that much. *Nothing's wrong. I'm fine, see?* She wanted to lie, even if it was painfully obvious. She wanted to console her, to apologise to him, but simply couldn't find the drive to pick herself up from the floor and continue along with her life.

It was her mantra. *I'm fine.* Over and over again. *I'm fine.* Every time she thought it, *I'm fine,* every time it played back in her mind, *I'm fine,* she forgot more, more, and yet more about the situation that disproved her claims. *I'm fine.*

At that, her body laid in dormancy for the next few minutes to transpire, stilled by shock, in spite of her racing mind. The spitting image of true, undeniable disappointment. Once a kind, silent yet respectable woman, reduced to the child she dreamed she was, her mind empty, and yet full, blank for reason, and yet vehement with thoughts, white, and yet black. Foolish to put trust in, and more foolish yet to trust others. Somebody who hadn't changed, even after convincing themselves they had developed so much over the course of their studies. Somebody that nobody batted their eyes at, raised their noses to, or thought about at all. A nobody.

Not even someone who had given up on life, or someone who had – put simply – gone insane and lost the plot completely. She was just a nobody.

Interlude I.

A Time long forgotten

"We were inseparable. Every second we could, we would spend together. There isn't a moment in my mind that I can think of, in which we had been apart."

"She only kissed Diana Pfeffermille 'cause she was gonna pay her! Get off 'er case!" Penelope barked at the murder of boys before them, cawing ruthlessly at the poor, shivering woman by their side. "*Jesus,* it's like y'all were born from a slab of cement and a damned pebble! Jus' leave the poor girl be!"

"Oh yeah? And we're supposed to believe that after sleeping in Friedrich Ludwig's accom' a couple weeks ago? Don't make me laugh!" The leader of the group, Christopher McScheiller (a relatively physically fit, well-known 'mean kid', and definitely not a force to be reckoned with) called out to the group sardonically, a hand on his hip as he tossed his head back, writhing in the pleasure of Violet's anguish and pain. "We all know who that girl is; she hangs around with yids like him, and trannies and queers like you!" They squealed out mockingly, like a farm of pigs all bathing in the mud together, tormenting the woman, who stood emotionlessly in the corridor with a rather hieroglyphic expression plastered on her face.

'I'm sorry, we should go. I didn't mean to cause trouble…' She raised her hands and signed to Penny, who shook their head as they leaned down to whisper secretively into Violet's ear. Their voice had become scarily calm, as if they were plotting something, though wouldn't reveal it to the auburn-haired woman beside them, in the fear that she would rat them out.

"No."

'Why not?' She signed again, in true silence, as she always was.

"All I'm gonn' say is, these fuckers had it a *looong* time comin'." Unbuttoning the cuffs of their sleeves to roll them up, Violet was rather slow to catch on to her plans; much to Penelope's advantage; as she silently watched the angelic, yet still rather strange, hero step up to Joshua's height. "Hey, punk!" They called out aimlessly, for the gang of giggling hyenas to stare up at them, bewildered, a few erupting into their characteristic, notable, shrill giggles as they set each other off. "I dunno why y'all are laughin', 'less y'all wanna get yer asses whooped even harder," they screamed again, tearing through the group's incessant screeches of joy, competing for vocal dominance with them all. It almost seemed impossible, and yet, here they were, doing it all single-handedly to defend a poor freshie they had never met before.

Violet began to recoil at their aggression, her hands curling up at her chest, tote bag swinging awkwardly beside her body as she stepped back a little, smoothing a hand over her school skirt. She wore her pencil skirt in the most proper manner the school recommended; down to her knees – or, well, slightly raised above – so that it tapered to the ends of her thighs, in a fashion that when she stepped one could imagine a bell chiming with each slow tap of her heel; and yet, the only thing chiming was her constant, loud mind, screaming at itself and cowering in fear at its own power.

Why are you letting this random person defend you? Fight your own battles for once. You look like a child, needing people to constantly help you win fights and arguments because you can't cope.

I can't. I can't do it. I'm sorry.

You're going to get torn up, eaten, puked, and thrown back onto the street in five minutes flat with that attitude.

I'm fine. I would have been fine. I didn't want to cause trouble.

Obviously. They wanted to cause trouble. You're the one who got caught in the middle of it all.

We both know that.

Then why don't you fight back? Get angry! Scream! Fight! Break their bones! Crack their skulls! Give them a taste of their own medicine! Remind them of their own humanity!

There is good inside everything. I know that much.

Are you even listening to me?!

Of course not. Why should I? You only care for violence, anger, how many punches it takes to knock out someone's lightbulb. What sense do you have for me to pry into?

But don't you think, even for one second, that these people deserve it? Didn't you pay $160 for all of those textbooks they just set fire to? What about your uniform, that mother ironed for you just for your first day of school?

What goes around will eventually come back to them. I'm fine.

What about Mi—

Stop it. I'm fine.

Snapping out of her trance, she felt the heat on her body. Clinging to her like moths to a flame, like the sweat to her skin. Like him. *Stop thinking about him. He is the exception,* she didn't say out loud, but hissed at her active mind, as if to shut the two forces raving on about something or other inside of it, simply standing by to watch Penelope fight whoever had decided to bully her this time. Punches, kicks, right-hooks, left-hooks, she'd name it and Penny would deliver. It was just about as if Penny could read her thoughts and acted upon her will. A ridiculous thought, true, but just about plausible.

'Excuse me,' she tried to sign, moving to tap Penelope on the shoulder in futility, until the neatly straightened collar had all of its pressing work undone by the individual she was trying to grab the attention of, as they gripped onto it aggressively. As soon as their mind had caught up with their hands, they made haste in putting her down gently, giving one final kick to every member of Joshua's posse, then spitting down at them all harshly. The saliva landed just beside the leader's face – lucky for him – but it only caused a disappointed glower to overtake Penny's face, staring the black-and-blue group down in disdain.

"Leave us alone." They grumbled, taking Violet's hand and walking her away from the rather gruesome, unholy scene. Yeah, as if whatever God was up there was sitting in a cinema booth with a box of popcorn in His right hand. "Hey, are ya' doin' okay?" They had asked it as more of a courtesy rather than a genuine inquiry; it was rather easy to tell that she wasn't, but it felt wrong not to ask.

'I'm fine,' she broke from the grasp that the salmon pink-haired person had on her, moving to leave until Penny yanked her back.

"No, y'aint," retorted Penelope, glaring at her sternly as they continually rambled on, "I just saw ya' get'cher ass absolutely, undeniably *beaten ta' shit* by Joshua and his cronies. Yer *not* fine, an' I reckon we both know that." Looking up at them with glossed-over eyes, like resin had been poured over each ball to really emphasise her sorrow, Violet turned her head away and refused to look at the good Samaritan before them any longer. Uncourteous of her, sure, but she had reason to look away.

'I didn't need your help. *You*, of all people, don't exactly make my case any better.'

"And why's that, if I may ask?" They stood to their full height, painfully aware of why Violet had signed what she had, but still curious as to what excuse she would pull out of her ass. Her challenging expression sized Violet up and down, an eyebrow cocked upwards in suspicion. "Or is Miss 'got-fucked-up-by-the-textbook-bullies-but-doesn't-need-help' too rude to bother?"

Rude. The cheek of it all, Violet's racing mind spat venom at Penelope, but she didn't dare speak out loud to her. She held herself back, for now. 'Now, I don't personally have anything against your presentation; quite frankly, it's none of my business and I don't care' – she raised a hand to pause Penny and their train of thought as their maw unhinged to begin to argue her previous claims – 'until it concerns me, which it absolutely does, before you start; but the fact that you are what many consider to be a transgender individual is seriously damaging my image.'

Penny took a moment to think. "... Dont'cha go forgettin' that'cha *did* kiss Diana Pfeffermille— who, by the way, is basically the *gayest* girl in the whole ding-dang school, 'sides me— so now everyone thinks *yer* a queer, too." Penelope folded their arms at the claims that Violet had made, leaning down in a slight hunch again as they reminded her of the burning humiliation that she had sustained a few days prior, watching as her expression shrivelled up in disgust. "So, I guess the real thing I'm try'na ask is *are* ya' a queer?"

A beat of silence passed them both, Violet's eyebrows tightening as they pulled themselves closer together, threatening to meet between her eyes as she formulated an answer mentally. 'That's none of your business,' concluded Violet, watching as the older student in front of her – they had to, at the very least, be a sophomore compared to her – sized her up and down, as if her eyes were scanning her intently.

"Y'know, I 'ain't gonna tell nobody. 'Ain't no point in outin' ya to the whole school…" Penny's voice quietened down for a moment, "seein' as most of 'em already know…" They then raised their voice to its normal, peppy volume, arms crossing tighter, yet still in a bubbly fashion. They quite clearly had no ill-intent toward Violet, but still found her interesting to debate with, nonetheless. "What I'm try'na say is ya' don't gotta hide that shit 'round me. I don't care; I'm gonn' find out sooner or later. Might as well tell me now – queer to queer."

'Again,' after a long while of thinking to herself, Violet continually signed, refusing to make eye contact with the individual before her, hands trembling as she tried to keep her signs legible, 'that's *still* none of your business. I don't see any reason that you want to pry into this. I'm not like *you.*'

"Oh, but'cha are, Violet." Before the woman could turn on her heel, Penny called out to her with a more sympathetic look plastered on their face, onlooking the girl who had sped up to avoid the inevitable conversation the older of the two was going to bring onto her. "Ya' can't hide it forever! Trust me, I've tried."

And, perhaps, for the passing moment that Violet stopped in her tracks, she was right. Perhaps, they were a little more similar than she once stopped to ponder and dismiss. Perhaps, hypothetically speaking, she would turn around and confess everything, that she was a queer and she wanted to kiss girls, or boys, or anyone that would kiss her back instead of running away in fear or disgust.

She concluded that discussing hypotheticals was pointless and turned away from the idea along with moving as far away from Penny as she could. After all, she was fine the way she was.

'I'm fine.' She signed it over her head, just high enough for Penelope to see, even if she had to squint to interpret the signs.

Stage III.

Guilt

"She didn't leave her room for days after her parents came. I don't know what happened to her, or what sort of demons got into her to make her isolate herself, but it was… almost dystopian to see from an outsider's perspective."

It was late. Almost too late, but not quite. Simply late.

Heaving herself out of the cocoon she had formed on the couch out of blankets, pillows and the numerous amounts of clothes she wore, Violet gripped the remote in her hands, threatening to turn off the TV – it was playing a melodrama of sorts about losing a friend to drugs or something of the sort – but stayed calm and sat herself down to watch it properly.

Wow. How fitting for what's just happened.

Turn it off.

Why should I? Do you really want to forget what went down that quickly?

You don't even know how she died. Turn it off.

It could have been like this. Maybe a car crash. Maybe suicide. Maybe murder.

Maybe she's not even dead and this is all a sick joke.

Yes, true, but why would he have given you the letter confirming her death if not?

Why would he have scribbled out the cause of death?

To protect me. Turn it off.

To <u>hurt</u> me. That's all he ever does.

I don't care. This is serious and he wouldn't lie about something like this.

Stop being so naïve. Of course, he would. He's <u>Michael</u>. There's not a thing in the world he wouldn't do to get something out of you.

I concur; however, this issue is important. Even <u>he</u> wouldn't lie about something like this.

How can you be so sure?

Turn the TV off.

Why should I?

<u>Turn it off</u>.

Her hands begin to tremble, curling around the remote in a mighty grip. Her mind continued to bicker with itself.

What are you going to do if I don't?

I don't know, but it's not going to end well.

Are you gonna cry?

Turn it off.

Are you gonna cry, little baby? You don't have Penelope to fight for you anymore. They're not gonna come and coddle you and tell you you're fine when you both know you're not—

Turn. It. Off.

—and when you come crying to your parents, they are gonna cut you to ribbons—

Turn the damn TV off!

—and this is just like that time when Joshua rocked your shit big-time 'cause you're a damn queer and they came to save you from your own ineptitude, and you shoved them away like a heartless piece of shit—

I said turn it off!

Involuntarily, Violet woke up from her trance-like state, gaining a sudden awareness of the world around her. Noticing the shattered glasses on the table, the tears dripping from her eyes, the way her mouth had downturned into an enraged grimace and the lack of remote in her hands, seeing as it was wedged into the broken screen of the television. "Oh." The sound left her lips quietly, as if it had just stumbled out on accident, leaving her speechless again as she took more note of what had just transpired.

She didn't even realise it had happened, and yet she had gone and given herself more chores to do anyway; regardless of whether 'she' had done it or not, she continued to ignore the fighting and arguing in her subconscious as she reached for the paper towels, stood on the table proudly. In the moments that she tried to quell the internal violence festering within her, she kept repeating her mantra. Over, and over, and over. *I'm fine. Turn it off. He did it to protect me. You don't even know how she died. She's not even dead, it's a sick joke. I'm fine. He did it to protect me. Turn it off. You don't even know how she died. I'm fine. I'm fine. Turn it off.*

Walking back over to the scene of her unbridled rage, she began to gently pick up tiny shards of the glass cup she was drinking out of, prior to her accident, placing the small flakes and chips into her hand, protected by the square of paper towel she had rather aggressively torn away from the roll. It almost reminded her of him. *He did it to protect me. I'm fine. He did it to protect me. Turn it off.* Balling up the broken glass, she walked back over to the TV, her hands still clammed up from God knows whatever she had done before she had woken up, in a sense.

You don't even know how she died. Her eyes moved over the shattered surface of the television screen, shoulders initially raising in a horrid yet confused flinch, as if she had remembered something she didn't have a memory of. *I'm fine.* Standing up taller, trying to best the might of her fears, she pulled away the blankets from the couch to search for more pieces of glass, concluding her search and moving back into the kitchen lifelessly to rip another fistful of paper towel away from the roll and descend to her knees in front of the TV, hands still shaking.

Do you even want to know what happened?

Of course, I do.

Why?

For peace of mind.

A third voice interrupts her internal conflict. *I'm fine.*

Michael was right. This will only make you worse off.

No, he wasn't. He's <u>never</u> right. You are foolish for even conceiving the thought.

Turn it off.

But you did too, no? We are facets of one mind. If I thought it, you thought it.

You don't even know how she died.

Don't be ridiculous. I don't associate myself with your impulsivity and intrusiveness.

He did it to protect me.

You would be nothing without me. Someone with no flaws or fears is a shell of a person.

Turn it off.

Someone with no flaws or fears is <u>happy</u>.

That isn't true.

I'm fine.

"Jesus," mumbled out Violet, maybe to break the unbearably loud silence, clasping a hand over her left ear as if to rip out the dagger the quiet had driven through her head, shaking herself off and continuing to collect up all of the glass she had involuntarily broken. Shard after shard, speck after speck, sliver after sliver. Once she was done, as she had before, she returned to the kitchen to dump it all in her trash bin. *I'm fine.* Immediately moving away, like she was trying to avoid the thought, she murmured something or other to herself and sat down on the couch in silence again.

Now, she was alone with her thoughts. *Alone* alone. Nothing to stop herself from thinking. Nothing to inhibit every last intrusive thought racing for dominance in the very seconds she was spending focusing on them. Standing up after she got sick of sitting in silence for a minute or maybe two or potentially even three – she had lost track of the disparity between them all – she carried herself lazily to the payphone on the table, beside the door, where it had always been, dialling a number and listening in to the droning ring.

"Hello? Ludwig Residence?"

"Why did you call my parents?" Her voice wasn't inquisitive in the slightest, more venomous and just about harmful than anything else. The spite that she spat was palpable. "Why didn't *you* come here? Why did you send *them,* of all people?"

"I didn't want to get involved. I know what you're like when you're like this." Friedrich answered, hesitantly, trying not to enrage, upset or set her off further.

"What's that supposed to mean?"

"You're grieving."

"And you can't even think for one minute to support me? Your *friend?*"

"You don't need my support. You need to take a good, long look at yourself and process this information in a healthy way. You need your family, more than you need me."

Silence, for just the passing moment.

"Fuck you, Dr. Ludwig."

"Why?" He asked, almost as if to poke a dead horse, to see if it'd move. Just an odd bit of curiosity; inquisitiveness was always a personality quirk of his.

"What do you mean," began Violet, "why?" She hissed not long after, taking in a deep breath, "you *lied* to me and sent my parents after me. Don't I have a right to be angry? Don't I have a right to tell you to fuck off?"

"I did it for your own good."

"You did it because you don't want to help me." She seethed back at him, with no energy to enable his behaviour. Her hatred was boiling and frothing, ready to spill out and coat her entirely in an unstoppable, relentless fire. "You think

I'm some sort of fucking lost cause?! You want me to give you lost cause?!"

"You know," Friedrich began, in the same calm tone as ever, "you sound just like your brother."

Oh my God.

Putting the phone down, hand shaking with a horrid tremor, she stumbled backwards, then began to distance herself from the object as far as she could. Racing upstairs, she settled into the covers of her bed, shielding her head from any external attackers, despite her ineptitude in protecting herself from those on the inside.

You're just like your brother.

I'm fine.

Get a hold of yourself!

Why should I?! Why do you, of all people, suddenly care about my well-being?!

<u>*Because I am you*</u>*!*

I'm fine. Turn it off.

Get lost.

You don't even know how she died.

I don't need to. I have a right to be angry.

You're angry because you don't know.

I'm angry because everyone is withholding information from me.

So, yes?

If it will make you shut the Hell up, then, yes.

I'm not going anywhere.

I know that. I'm fine.

Stop repeating things. You're throwing me off.

She's not even dead, it's a sick joke.

You're sick.

I'm fine.

You are <u>not</u> fine. Quit trying to lie and convince yourself that you're fine, all of the time. You're not. You never have been. Just because other people say you're fine doesn't make it true. You're broken. Damaged. Impaired. Deformed. You're anything but fine.

I'm fine.

That's what he said when he came home with a shiner and a broken arm when mother and father went on their honeymoon—

Stupid fucking Michael.

—and you had to nick him super gently, just the way you taught them to do it after the fight with Josh—

Stupid fucking Penny.

—when they called you faggy queers, just like the queer you are, because you kissed Diana Pfeffermille behind the bleachers and slept at Friedrich's place because you didn't feel safe after he called you again—

Stupid fucking Josh. Stupid fucking Diana. Stupid fucking Friedrich.

—and you sat in your dorm, crying like a bitch. Because they told you the <u>truth</u>, that you hang out with kykes and queers. And you said you were fine. When you knew you weren't, you said you were fine. You didn't think you had a right to not be fine, because you didn't think you were the victim.

Stupid fucking dorm.

She had noted this new part of her mantra down; anything she wanted to curse mentally, whether that be her brother, or best friend, or first girl-kiss, or high-school bully, or another best friend; and decided to repeat that over and over to challenge her rational mind. She had no time or room for rationality. She only felt an unbearable rage for the world around her but decided to sleep on it. She didn't care much for expressing anger when nobody was around to give her the attention she was desperately crying out for.

That was normally how she got what she wanted. Sobbing, crying, screaming. She didn't do it often, seeing as she didn't want much, and lived a simple life with her brother and parents, but sometimes the fact that he got so much praise for doing so little just pricked at her the wrong way.

How did he get away with being the stupid kid, the artsy, sporty kid, the kid who always got everything he asked for, the kid who got to express himself, when she was stuck being the kid who had to have A+ grades in every subject in every report card, the smart kid, the know-it-all kid, the freak kid, the 'just say something you weirdo' kid, the 'why don't you just talk instead of throwing up those gang signs' kid, the 'why do you need a notebook to communicate with us just say something you fucking freak' kid, the 'Michael you're gonna get really badly hurt one day and I won't be there to take care of you' kid, the kid who only hangs out with 'kykes and dykes' because they're the only kids who want her around?

All manner of questions began to pick away at her, forcing her to lay herself in her bed and writhe in the disgust of exhaustion. She had always hated it, just the same as how she felt about the people around her – it served no purpose other than to hold her back. Maybe the solution was enjoyable and somewhat necessary for a while, but people could live, and had lived, without it. The only problem was the fact that all of the actions leading up to the exhaustion, to the loneliness, had each and every individual action and consequence to account for.

Perhaps a cup of tea she had to make, or another problematic thing to say to get someone to leave her alone, or the washing-up she hadn't gotten around to doing yet because she was procrastinating on it, or just something to get them away from her because she didn't care what it needed to be – it just needed to be something bad, or mopping the kitchen tiles because she couldn't see her reflection in them anymore and the untidy tiles bothered her immensely, or kissing Diana Pfeffermille behind the bleachers so everyone would see her for the dirty queer she was and finally leave her alone were all indisputable examples of consequences she had to face to reach her goal, whether it be a clean house and avoiding sleep, or near total isolation.

Stage IV.

Anger

"Then came outbursts, rage, just– an inconceivable level of true anger at the world. It was so… strange, to just watch it happen. All I could do was watch, as she fell apart."

'Just the tea, please.' Her handwriting was neat, poise and perfect, as it had always been; though, surprisingly so, for the situation she had been planted in for the past two weeks. She had focused more on forcing herself out of the house – a long enough distraction would have satisfied her craving to reach into her chest and pull apart all the pulsating, disgusting flesh to reach her heart and savagely rip it out, prying past all of the bones guarding it to throw it onto the floor and join them in–

"That'll be $5.45, darlin'." The voice snapped Violet out of her gruesome thoughts, head whipping up to see the barista, hand open for the change she would eventually place into her palm. Watching as she walked away, she couldn't hold back the thoughts of a carnal rage inside of her, burning her throat and causing a horrid shiver to run down her spine, the spine she wanted to break out of her own back in an uncharacteristic, untameable anger–

"Hey, get out'ta the way! We're waiting to order here, lady!" The jeers, once again, forced her into an increased awareness of the world around her, causing her head to lift from its originally bowed position as she plodded over to the waiting desk, hitting her back to the wall. Part of her wished she would fall through, that the old, crumbling paint would simply cave in and the bricks would pile up beneath her, almost in a futile attempt to cushion her fall as she tumbled to the pavement.

What the hell is wrong with you? Shooing the thoughts away with a passing of her hand through the fiery locks of her hair – fire she wished to burn her – she drew her hands over her arms again – arms she wished to scratch all of the skin off – to seat on her hips – hips she wished to break apart like a collection of building blocks to place back together in her desire, or perhaps leave alone to rot away in the millions of years it would take her carbon-based bones to decompose and become a fossil fuel to burn away and turn into the atmosphere. To continue the cycle of pain from one person to another. Perhaps, to even transfer it to the person about to suffer from a horrid cough, or the gaping hole in the ozone layer that her carbon-based species had created.

Oh, how she wished to rid herself of it all. What 'it all' consisted of was beyond her; maybe it concerned her life, or other people's lives – those that troubled her, at least – or everything. Maybe it concerned this café, starting with burning it to the ground, with a single match or a dousing of gasoline and watching the old walls and the crumbling paint go up in flames, the same fiery flames that her hair possessed the colour of, or maybe it was the people in the café that she wanted to rid herself of, how she wanted to grip the barista by her dirty-blonde pigtails and slam her head into the waiting desk, how she wanted to see the blood drip down her forehead as she fell limp under her grasp, how her eyes would roll up in a lack of further consciousness–

"Violet? Order for Violet?"

"Oh," she mumbled meekly, swallowing her internal conflict, forcing it to stay internal in the fear it might have become external, lest she realized she had free will. Raising her hand in a rather awkward manner, she took the cup before that same, jarring, grating voice called out to her.

"Hey," the barista began, waving a different employee to take over the till as Violet spun on her heel, eyebrow raised as she walked back over with a mild intrigue. Whatever this barista wanted had to be important. "I noticed that you didn't say anything to me. Talkin' with the notepad," she gestured to the A5 book, bound with a metal spiral, tucked under Violet's arm, and the pen, neatly seated within the peals of Violet's hair, settled comfortably against her ear. "Just a simple bit'a curiosity's all I'm getting at here. What's up with it?"

Taking in a deep breath, Violet couldn't begin to articulate her thoughts, let alone how the murderous kind only strengthened with how nonchalant this *complete stranger,* she reminded herself, suddenly felt entitled to an inquiry on her personal situation of selective mutism. Gently slipping her notebook from underneath her arm, she took her pen from behind her ear, clicking it once and beginning to write.

'I have selective mutism.' She wrote, simple and short, then tore it off to hand to the barista, taking her tea in hand until that jarring, grating voice yelled out for her again. She could have sworn she felt the burning trickle down her hand, the paper cup curling beneath her iron-gripped clenching, the fist threatening to form in the palm of her beverage but refusing to ruin the perfectly good hot drink she had just paid the insufferable woman for.

"Hey, wait up!" The barista yelled out again, ignoring the utter discomfort and internal agony on Violet's face, stepping over the waiting desk to catch up to her. "I never got your name," she huffed tiredly, laughing a little as she placed a hand on Violet's shoulder. The subsequent flinch and pulling away of the woman, now a few paces away, was enough to shut her up. Violet nodded to her – not as a mannerism of respect or acknowledgement, more in absolute and unadulterated disgust – and walked off, trying her best not to spin on her heel and send a left hook flying directly into the barista's face.

I'm fine.

You should have punched her right to Albuquerque.

Stop it. I'm fine. She didn't do anything wrong; it's like she said, a simple bit of curiosity.

Curiosity killed the cat.

But satisfaction brought it back?

That wasn't part of the saying.

How do you know?

God, you just don't <u>shut up</u>, do you?

If I did, you'd be talking to yourself right now.

That doesn't matter. Internal monologues are <u>mono</u>logues. I'm fine. Everything is fine. Why am I thinking like this? Why do I suddenly want to hurt people? Should I see a doctor? No– I'm fine. I don't need a doctor, let alone the hospital bills. I just want an excuse to go and get the attention I'm desperate for, don't I? Isn't that right? God,

I'm pathetic. Am I seriously that disconnected from reality? Hey... is anyone even listening to me? Hello?

Blinking a little as she found herself deep in the woods, with nothing but a notebook, a pen and a cup of tea that had just about slipped out the most marginal spillage of tea over her trembling fingertips, she tried her best to gather her bearings and follow her footsteps back. She did happen upon her house, after ten minutes or so of walking, but found herself still perplexed as to how she had ended up so deep in the forest. She had *never* gone that deep into the forest.

Opening the door to her house, she almost felt a surreal urge fill her veins, pouring through her mind, like she wanted to rip the wood away from its metal hinges and toss it forty miles across the wide expanse of the forest, to hear the sound of the trees thudding and confirm she was there to listen out for the deafening crash, or maybe to slam her own head into the beams of carbon-based wood holding her door as the familiar structure it'd be recognized as, to feel her body drain of the blood she needed to survive and her body to fall limp against the door. Her corpse would be a horrid sight, no doubt, vile and disgusting and sickening and anybody who came across it sure would say it was a sorry sight to see.

Taking the first few steps into her hallway was enough of a difficult feat as it came upon her, but she continually, consistently ignored the unnatural urges, primal and clawing at the fabric of her mind, its claws threatening to tear through and spill blood wherever it saw fit, simply to dump her bags onto the couch she had sat on for the past two weeks, staring contemplatively into her broken TV and wondering what on Earth she was to do next. If she continued the way she was walking now, God knew how deep into the forest – or, rather, her mind – she would wander, or how much of her surroundings would be destroyed by her cardinal wrath.

Standing to walk to the kitchen, with each floorboard squealing out for help beneath her step, she wished they would all cave through, with not only a satisfying crackle and a crumble but a true tearing-apart and showing-what-for, designed specifically to force them all into the submission of whatever she was planning to get them to fall apart under her rage, and then perhaps she would hit her head on a slab of cement, or she would plummet through to the centre of the Earth, or just something, *anything,* that would get her out of the Hellhole she was forced to live in, out of the rat race she was forced to run, out of the life she was forced to lead.

Jesus Christ, you're dramatic.

I'm you.

Get a hold of yourself. Do you seriously think torturing and killing yourself is going to make anything better? If I knew any better, I'd just get <u>him</u> to come and torment you more, seeing as you want that so badly.

No. I'm fine. It must be on my own volition.

Why? Are you scared he's going to do more than you want him to?

I'm not scared. He may have scared me in the past, but he holds no dominion over me now. I have no reason to fear him.

Are you saying he should fear you?

Perhaps, I am. So, what, if I am?

Why?

Because he–... Why are you asking this question? You are me. You know everything he's done to me. What is the point in this string of pointless queries?

Introspectivity.

My point being, I don't want him to hurt me anymore. I don't want to hurt others, or myself.

Then what <u>do</u> you want?

I want <u>them</u>. We both know I want them.

Death is a part of life. There is no getting them back, and we both know that.

But can we not dream?

We can, but dreaming is pointless. Why dream of something you know will never come true?

Dreams don't have to come true. Perhaps… they can be just 'dreams'. A far-away thought, a concept that we wish to be true, but we know won't ever happen. Is that not intrinsically what a dream is?

... Why are you doing this?

Pausing her ingrained tea-making – forgetting entirely about the tea she had bought – in which she practically didn't even have to pay attention to, which gave her a greater span of time to ponder her own existence and sorrow, she placed her cup down lifelessly, moving over to the drawer and dipping her hand into the open furniture to pull out a spoon. Her hand glided over the kitchen knives, seated neatly between each other, just itching to be plucked away from the comfort of the plastic they stayed sorted in, though she once again disregarded the urge to grab the knife by the handle, unsteady and shaky in her movements, then plunge it not once, but perhaps twice or even three times – if she still had the consciousness to do so – into her chest, abdomen, arms, legs, wherever she saw fit, wherever would kill her fastest, to lose the ability to live moments later as it seeped from the holes she had forced into her body, and to drop the knife to the floor with a sonorous clang as her knees buckle inwards, to hit her head on the counter and fall limp on the linoleum floor she stood on right that very second–

Jesus Christ. She took a few, fearful paces away from the drawer, shutting it with the lifting of her foot to nudge it back into place wearily, dropping the spoon into the mug full of freshly brewed tea, stirring once or twice and then straining the tea bag to throw into the pile of fermenting Earl Grey tea bags by the microwave, sitting at the round table in the centre of her kitchen. Refusing to admit to herself that she was in severe, dire need of help, Violet began to ponder the less than pleasant interaction of the early morning she had been given the untimely joy of experiencing. *Stupid fucking barista. I can't believe she had the nerve – the cheek! – to try and call me back after I had made it pretty clear I didn't want anything to do with her–*

That's not fair to say that. She could have been like them. You don't know that.

I think I'd be able to tell.

Would you? You couldn't tell with Penny until they told you.

That doesn't matter. That was different. They were different.

Different to you?

Yes. Very different to me.

But not different enough for you to dislike them?

I could never dislike them.

But you did, at some point, did you not?

That was in the past. I was ignorant, and I was a fool.

Who is to say you aren't still ignorant now?

What do you want me to do, go and apologise to the barista for doing practically nothing?

Perhaps, you need to consider how you view people before forming instantaneous opinions on strangers.

Taking a sip of her tea, silent and poised, as she naturally was, she continued to think and debate with her inner consciousness.

I don't need to consider anything.

Many would consider you an unpleasant person for that.

So be it. It's not like this will get any worse.

I severely doubt that.

Opening her eyes just that little bit wider after lifting her head from its naturally bowed position, she took a slight look around her home for a moment. This *could* get worse. This could *definitely* get worse. And the worst part of how much worse this could get was the fact that she had no clue how much worse it would get or what on God's green and bountiful Earth could make it so much worse. All she knew for certain was the fact that this not only wasn't the end of how much worse it was potentially going to get, but it sure as Hell wasn't the end of it.

Sitting up straight and waking herself from her own mind with the ringing of her spoon in the cup, rattling incessantly to force her out of her debilitating thoughts, she picked it out of the murky brown liquid and settled into the cushion beneath her further, disconcerted by the amount of harmful thoughts seeping into her brain. Before she could even conceive the thought of tearing her brain out from between the plates of her skull, she took another long, hard sip of her tea, focusing closely on how it burned each of her tastebuds, disregarding it as a mere method of distraction from whatever was troubling her so greatly.

Of course, she had a very strong feeling about what was causing the fray within her mind; she had the inkling that she had gotten the short end of the stick, the worst of the worst that could somehow potentially still get worse, the absolute bottom of the barrel and perhaps not even that, perhaps she had just gotten the barnacles and repressed childhood memories and horrid experiences and development she had experienced over the course of her life with Penelope lumped together and slapped within her begging, scarred palms.

Those barnacles, that lump, was thrown carelessly into those same palms, palms curled with thorns and roses, with individuals hovering around her to drip water and plant-food steadily onto the sweet pain she was experiencing, that were once again being forced into her hands with the weight of the metaphorical barnacles she had not two weeks ago been given by her dear brother, carrying the weight upon his own palms free of thorns and vines and beautiful, blood-red, carnelian roses with petals scattered around his form. Of course, as he always was in his time, he was being aided by her parents – that was no shock to her, it never had been – but also her old friends, and his old friends, and the barista, and the knives in the drawer, and everything that could pose the slightest potential for a threat to her existence.

Anything that had hurt her in the past had ample opportunity to do its worst now.

Interlude II.

Old Habits die Hard

"Every single time I brought it up, she would adamantly refuse it. I can't help but wonder where she learned it from."

"Violet, my dear," her mother began, caressing her daughter's updo, littered with ringlets and curls and peals of fiery ginger hair, "you must start to consider a suitor soon. You're coming to that beautiful age," she sighed softly, in reminiscence of her own childhood days, clearly seeing herself in her child, as if Violet was merely a mirror image of her mother. Beginning her ramble again, her mother was quick in continuing her previous sentence, with no intention of stopping the lecture, "the age where boys become men and girls become women."

"Father says girls are ruined too soon by marriage and motherhood," she mumbled out, just as her mother removed the first hot roller from her hair, wincing at the tug on each individual strand that had already made her scalp rather sore.

She couldn't help but believe her father – a rare happenstance, indeed – seeing as she didn't want to be 'ruined', in his words. Perhaps he was trying to scare her into choosing the right individual, but she didn't want to fall into an endless, bottomless hole of poor choices, starting with her lover.

"Don't be ridiculous, my dear. Motherhood is a wonderful gift given to all women!" Rhythmically pulling her frail hands through Violet's curls, moving the tight rings into soft waves cascading down her clothed back, she continued to ramble on to her daughter aimlessly. "You'll understand soon enough." Placing her palm on Violet's hair, smiling warmly at her reflection in the mirror before parting her fringe ever so slightly, her mother parted her own lips to speak once more, "I know I did. Your brother and you are a wonderful addition to my life."

"Is that true?" Violet questioned, innocent as ever, frowning a little as she looked up at her mother. The benevolent glisten in their eyes that they shared were so alike and different, so akin and separate. Violet had clearly inherited her kindness from her mother, though the extent to which the younger LaFramboise showed it was clearly much larger than that of her mother. "Father says I'm socially inept. He wishes that I was more like Michael."

Sighing at her suddenly saddened lips, curled downward into a frown, Violet's mother took her comb and began to gently interleave it through each fire-orange lock, still talking on to her daughter endlessly. "Vincent is… fickle. His love is capricious and ever-changing, and I'm sure he only said that to get a reaction out of you. I know that your brother inherited it from him; you know how to deal with your brother, don't you?" Smiling down at her daughter with lidded eyes, the hazy light around her mother almost made her look like an angel, as if she used to be God's favourite, but was cast out from the group, for perhaps a more negative than positive reason.

"Yes," Violet answered poignantly, hands folded in her lap, eyes closed to recite the same old sentence, the age-old solution to her ever-growing problem. From the number of times that she had been repeating the same concept to herself, it was practically ingrained into her tiny, naïve mind. "I should… um… I should ignore my brother, and respect my father, right…?" Searching for confirmation and consolation, her mother quickly came to her solace, for once.

"Exactly, my dear," she cooed, smoothing her hand down the younger's hair once more, bringing her own fragile hand to aid her musing, pressing each fingertip to her forehead, "your brother and father are people, and not only people, but our family." Sighing, then righting the girl's clothing just as a manner to fidget with something as she spoke, her mother still hadn't concluded her speech. "Plus,

69

this is good for you!" Cheering quietly with a false glee, she trailed her hands down Violet's face, smoothing each fingertip following her palm down her shoulders, fixated on the mirror. "There will never be any gain," she pinched her fingers together with a marginal amount of space between them before she continued, "without a *little* pain."

"But why do we need pain?" Violet, once again, as a young child typically would, inquired curiously, peering up at her mother with a soft, solemn expression, just as she was about to stand up.

"I think that's enough questions for today," the mother dismissed her child as if she was some sort of alien stranger, like she had never been closely associated with the girl in her life, waving her off lazily as she shut the door behind her. Violet, now in solitude in her room, still sat on the wooden stool in front of the mirror, couldn't help but peer at her attire in the reflection. A frilly dress, in a peachy pink, though it felt closer to white than anything else, coupled with a bonnet and appropriately lacy stockings, the whole outfit finalised with a pair of white small heels. She didn't feel much of any discomfort in it, but felt it didn't quite suit her, like she was always destined for something beyond nobility or land-owning or simply inheriting her family's name and estates.

For the few moments that she remained settled in the chair, she began to ponder it more. Was this really all there was to her life? To sit, and look pretty, and hopefully attract a nice, rich nobleman to spoil her for the years to come. But *why?* Was life really all that enjoyable and frivolous if she couldn't gain anything? What was there to gain when she already had it all? Was she simply to be ruined by a man, whisked away at seventeen nine years later, to simply be bred and sucked dry and discarded to live a sheltered life of solitude and regret?

Looking up at her reflection in the mirror, she began to take something more into account. She didn't have that same abusive, desperate to hurt ire in her eyes, like her father, or the ability to lie on command and pretend she cared about anything she was destined for, like her mother. Instead, the glimmer in her eyes trailed down her cheeks, following the curvature of her slightly pudgy, pink cheeks as it fell to the floor, causing a small pool of that same glimmer to appear beneath her. "I don't want to be noble anymore," she whimpered pathetically, to nobody in particular, and accordingly got no response from nobody in particular.

All she did was cry, as each bow in her hair came undone and floated gracefully to the floor, as the ties on her dress loosened with every twitch, as she stepped out of her small-heeled shoes, to stumble and meander around the room with every tear falling from her eyes forcing her deeper into a drowsy state. Before she had even realised it, she was slumped against a bookcase, an educational book about the anomalies of the universe pried open within her gloved hands, convincing herself slowly, with every word, diagram and notation that her eyes glazed over, that this was simply how life was meant to be. All of the knowledge she was gaining, whatever she learned from the hundreds of thousands upon hundreds of thousands of books and papers and theses that she read, was simply so her parents could boast her results to the other members of nobility they interacted with.

Of course, being regarded as only leverage by her peers and parents was difficult to grasp, and she had only just connected the dots now, like she had just discovered the constellation depicting her life, but she took it extremely well. In a sense, she didn't really care all that much – it didn't make much difference to her life, at that very moment – but it did make her wonder what else was out there for her again. If this life, the one she was destined for, was a life of sheltered views and unspoken emotions and sensitivity, but only to the extent that her husband would approve of, what else was there for her?

What was beyond the life of nobility and royalty, calling her name?

Snapping her head up from her book, she quickly tucked it under her arm, standing to her feet again and fixing herself in the mirror quickly, tying up her hair once again and stepping into her shoes, one by one, walking up to the balcony a few metres away from her, standing up against the wall and gazing upon the rolls of hills, with each beam of light shooting through the thick canopy of trees coating each mound. She had never gone to explore the forest – her parents warned that it was far too dangerous for a girl like her – but now? Now, she wanted to take the risk.

She wanted it more than ever. She wanted to leap from the balcony dramatically, and land into a pile of hay or leaves, and quickly shake it off as it pulled away all the frills and ribbons and pearls she hated so much, to be free in the forest, to run and play and roughhouse and get as far as she could away from the land that trapped her. That part of her, the facet of her life that wanted to break free into whatever lied before her, the unknown that screamed her name and begged on its hands and knees for her to take one of its own, for her to allow it to whisk her away into a garden of freedom and enchantment.

Yet, in the moment that she allowed herself to be encapsulated by the idea of a grand escape from the treacherous life she led, she couldn't help herself from flicking back to all the responsibilities lumped onto her hands. It almost felt like thorns, digging into her forearms and holding her down, sinking into the porcelain sheets of skin coating her body, the promise of release just within her grasp but the comfort of familiarity keeping her held down, the stasis of permanence eternal in her life.

That permanence, the idea that she would never escape her life in the jail she called her home – except the rusted, dingy bars were neatly carved, marble pillars, and the dirtied floors were cleaned until one's face would shine in them, and the dark, unwavering shadows refused to creep into the land conquered by light – ate away at her relentlessly, biting at her skull and scraping its unruly teeth against the bone, threatening to cave in the plates of her cranium and tear away her brain. Of course, she refused to tell anybody how she felt, lest the unladylike descriptions she provided would anger her family further than normal.

Despite being so torn about her potential escape from and imprisonment within her own home, she knew one thing for certain. She had not one doubt in her mind that this singular fact was true, and she trusted it more than any theorem or equation she could have ever hoped to learn in her life. She was destined for more.

Stage V.

Bargaining

"The church was what shocked me the most. I remember distinctly, the way she renounced Christianity. One could suppose she was destitute enough to turn back to old habits. After all, you can't teach an old dog new tricks."

"I accept the Lord as my God and saviour," clasping the rosary beads in her hands, painted a tiffany blue with cracks threatening to chip away the neat paintwork, she recited the prayers she could remember and referenced her small, leather handbook for the ones she couldn't. To give her the benefit of the doubt, Violet hadn't prayed in at least a decade, and at most two. She had always associated it with the stench of the wood stain on the pews, and the way the priest would ogle her overdeveloped body, and the manner in which her parents constantly berated her for shying away from him and everyone else and simply just wanting to go home – regardless, her opinions of Roman Catholicism and her experiences with such a faith were less than pleasant. However, she was willing to give it another try.

Standing to her feet from her once knelt position, her hands remaining intertwined with each finger lacing across each other nearly, she took a glance at the clock. It had been slightly scarred, a few scratches and once fallen onto the floor, but mostly in okay shape – all Violet cared about was the fact that she could still read the time: 9:30 AM. It had been a while since she had checked the date, having almost completely lost track as the days merged into one long blur, one long eternal day that never ended, where the sun never set and the moon never rose, where the events of her tragic loss never faded in her mind.

The church service would start at 10:30 AM. She had discovered a local church in the neighbouring town – seeing as she lived practically in the middle of nowhere – and planned to drive at about 10:00 AM. Perhaps the Lord would listen to her prayers, finally, after he had ignored her for years on end, after he had shushed and silenced her cries and pleas for help for all of eighteen years. Maybe he would find it in his omnibenevolent heart to answer her calls, for once.

Taking her purse from the table lazily, she pried it open with her hand gently, stuffing her keys, a few sticks of peppermint chewing-gum and her wallet into it, then buttoning it closed and looping her arm through it. Realising she needed to close the door, Violet hastily dug her hand within the confines of her purse again, drawing her keys from the assortment of belongings and closing it once again to settle at the table and bide her time for half an hour.

Do you really think this is going to help?

It got us through life until <u>them</u>. Wasn't everything fine, back then?

Was it?

I think so. We lived a very privileged life.

No, we didn't. We lived in an abusive household and a sheltered life. I hardly find that considerably privileged.

I'm fine. I turned out just fine, didn't I?

I have my doubts about that.

Why do you always oppose me?

Why do you think that converting is a good idea?

Because this will help us. He will help us, this time.

He didn't for eighteen years, when we were arguably <u>most</u> destitute. What difference does that make now?

It makes all the difference. He will listen to us this time, I'm sure.

If that's what helps you sleep at night.

It does.

Mumbling in disdain to herself, she pressed her palms to the plush couch cushions beneath her, littered with crumbs and flecks of glass and whatever else had imposed on her rage-filled rampage, maybe a few nights prior, or perhaps even a couple of weeks – again, she had lost track of the time ages ago, or maybe a week ago, since she couldn't tell for sure and refused to stare into her calendar to try and figure out what the day was. Perhaps she could ask someone in church.

One couldn't blame her for forgetting the day, or even the month, or maybe even the year; with the day that lived in her head on repeat, there was no other day, hour, minute or second that remained in her mind. She couldn't forget it. She *wouldn't* forget it. She would never let herself forget that day, that very second that her brother stepped into the house, the moment that he delivered the news, the hour she spent afterwards in tears and sorrow, the days that blurred into weeks that blurred into the month or so she had been living with that horrid memory.

She couldn't even begin to imagine what sort of pain that Penelope had gone through. She didn't even know how they had died. She couldn't conceive the concept of her even being dead, let alone how she had passed away. All she knew is that they were no longer on Earth, and most likely resided somewhere in Heaven, or God knows where, and she couldn't do anything about it.

Perhaps a prayer or two, a desperate cry for her too-soon-taken friend, or any amount of donations or good deeds she could think of would bring her back and finally restore her faith to its once strong, prosperous belief. For now, she still retained some level of doubt, but refused to acknowledge it in its entirety, preferring to live in wilful ignorance of how utterly desperate she was. Regardless of her doubts and prayers and whatever else her mind wanted to oppose with, she continued to try her best to recall the memory of each set prayer and anything else she wanted to tag on at the end.

Standing up from her previous residence on the couch, she piloted herself over to the kitchen to brew a cup of tea – not necessarily because she wanted to drink tea, but more to have something to do with her hands, rather than just leaving them shaking upon her lap or sunk into the creased cushions beneath her palms. She couldn't bear to be still any longer, so she went back to the routine she had taught herself from the moment she had let her first sip of tea hit her lips. Turning the kettle on and fishing the teabag out of the small hemp-bag she stored them in gave her ample time to return to her thoughts once again.

Why are you doing this?

I've already told you; this is good for us.

You're being ridiculous. We're <u>not</u> going.

Since when do you have any jurisdiction over what we do? We are going, whether you like it or not.

Give me a real reason as to why you're doing this.

Why should I?

Because I <u>am</u> you. I deserve to know. I deserve to have a say.

No, you don't. Your ideas always end up causing us more harm; it's what you are. You are everything I'm not.

But we're still halves of the same person. Can't we work together?

All you will do is oppose me. We are going to that church.

No.

What do you mean, 'no'? No to what?

Everything.

This is exactly why I never consult you. All you do is argue and advocate for the devil's argument and oppose me. If I had known any better, I wouldn't have contacted you in the first place.

I would have known that you're thinking about this anyway, and I would have opposed you regardless of my nature. This is not a good idea; can't you think, for one second, about the trauma she went through concerning Roman Catholicism? Don't you think that inviting all of that trauma back into her life is at least a little damaging?

Perhaps it is. Exposure therapy is proven to work, however. I still firmly believe that this is good for her.

You are delusional.

And so what if I am?

Please think for a moment.

That's all we can do. That's all we are. We are just thoughts. Different aspects – different facets – of one mind.

Sitting upright as she found herself settled at her kitchen table, tea in hand, Violet had finally woken up to her surroundings, despite being internally and externally exhausted. She almost felt forced to perform, even if it wasn't at her best, but didn't have the energy to fight the urge to collapse and never stand to her feet again.

I must get ready soon, she thought to herself actively, trying her dearest to shun the war in her mind, concealing it as if she were her parents concealing away a scandal on their business – perfectly, that is – finally raising herself up from her seated position. Taking a short glance at the clock, she turned to grab her bag before looking at the time once again.

11:00 PM.

She hadn't a clue what exactly she had done to reach the end of the mass before she could even leave the house. All she knew was that she was late. Far too late to hopefully get there for the last few minutes; late enough to arrive at the very end of the church ceremony and look an utter fool while doing it. Sighing to herself in distress, she settled into her chair once again, then allowing her body to fall limp as her head hit the desk with a thud. She could hear the clank of her mug, filled with tea, and the dripping of presumably the liquid behind her, but actively chose to ignore it, in favour of simply sitting at her kitchen table and wondering what the hell was wrong with her.

For the remarkably smart woman she was, she only possessed such intelligence academically. When it came to sociability, she was truly pathetic, with an ineptitude for making the necessary connections she had to, or even speaking, for that matter. Time and time again, in public settings, her father would berate her relentlessly on how she was 'simply far too shy' and how 'the decision to stay silent was utterly medieval' and 'why can't you be more like your brother' and 'at least one of you isn't socially inept' and 'I will not have my daughter stammering in front of hundreds of people' and 'don't give me those crocodile tears, that speech was awful and you know it' and 'you'd better pray to God for mercy' and–

"Damn it all!" The obscene swear left her mouth, and she slapped a palm over it not long after, in utter shock of her own rage. She felt a guilt pile up within her heart and caught herself sitting in the chair she was sat in prior, seeing as she was so blinded by unbridled anger that she had stood up without even realising it, to make sure she didn't hurt any of the belongings in the house, or herself. Taking in a few sharp breaths, she raised a shaking hand to hold her head for a moment, in utter disappointment for how the situation had developed.

Once again, ignoring the distress in her mind, she stood to her wobbly, weak feet and picked the cup from the floor, to cautiously place it into the sink and make sure it hadn't broken, then lazily tossed a towel to the floor. Stepping upon the rag of fabric, she dried the tea from the floor and too gripped the tea towel to throw it towards the sink, then dragging the shell of her body up to her room.

Each step onto the creaky floorboards leading to her stairs drew her ire more, but that thin outer layer of rage would without fail melt away into a deeper sorrow. Every inconvenience felt like another pin in the cushion of her brain, and each pin pushed another deeper in, or brushed against it to trigger even more pain in the organ. She couldn't stop herself from feeling this way, on account of not wanting to medically remove the pain in her mind, but simply grinned and bore with the mental agony she fought on a daily basis. After all, it could always get worse. She didn't know how, but she was certain it could.

Walking up the stairs at possibly the slowest pace she had ever gone at, she took the last step and found herself on the top floor of her house, with nothing to show for herself. She had just walked up not even a full flight of stairs. What sort of accomplishment was that supposed to be? Why did she feel relieved? It all felt pointless, in that moment where she had felt happy, some sort of joy igniting in her, at the fact that she had climbed some stairs. It almost seemed impossible, for a second or two, more so when she was at the bottom of the staircase and each step stared her down menacingly, waiting to be stepped on, waiting to squeal out between each dainty step she took.

Regardless of her strange fascination with her ability to walk up some stairs, she headed over to her room and aggressively threw any item of loose clothing or jewellery onto the vanity set she had beside her. Naturally, she was dressed in her Sunday best, but didn't see any point in wearing it now, considering her best had just gone to waste, on the basis that her time management skills were, as of current, the worst.

After she had thrown most of her clothing off, she then threw herself onto the bed and didn't even bother with the bedsheets, falling into a deep sleep as soon as her head hit the cheap, hard pillow she slept on.

Stage VI.

Distress

"Then, she lost it. She basically lost her mind. If it scared me, and I was just watching, I don't even want to think about what she was feeling. All I know is that she had just– completely lost her mind."

She was knelt on the floor, knees sunk into the carpet, hunched over her mirror. Every punch she delivered into the reflective surface introduced more cracks into the silvery pane, her reflection becoming more and more distorted as she slammed her fist into the mirror. She couldn't do anything but cry out visceral screams of despair, echoing through the empty home as she punched and punched and punched, punched until her hand bled, punched until her arm ached, and still punched.

All she could do at that point was punch. It was all she had left in her. To beat down whatever she could, to exercise whatever power over anything and anyone around her, helped her just that miniscule bit to remember she was still in control. She still had control. Just a little bit, but she still had it, and by God, she gripped onto it with a tight-fisted valour, to keep herself sane and not drift away into the bounds of psychopathy or go completely mad.

Violet could barely see past all the tears in her eyes, though she felt them upon her skin, streaking down her face in their thousands, following the old tracks like an orderly set of troops marching to war – or, perhaps, away from war – to fall upon the shattered mirror beneath her bent position. Each ball of saline fluid that left her eyes only brought an onslaught of ten more, like an exponential growth of sorrow marking her face with all it was worth. Her throat burned with the screams she was letting out, and her eyes stung with the tears she dared to cry, but she didn't think for one moment to stop. Perhaps, she didn't think at all.

She couldn't see the blood staining the mirror, either the way it pooled up and splattered against the shattered glass with every slam of her fist into the already broken mirror. Every drop of claret from inside her spilled by her capacious, indiscriminate rage slipped from beneath the layer of skin that protected her fell onto the mirror, to be lost within the cracks and sink behind the momentary safety of the glass, to prolong its life for just a few seconds more, until the tyrant that once harboured the blood would throw down another punch and send the liquid flying in all manner of directions. Anywhere, to get away from her.

There was no moment of clarity for her – not in this instance, at least. Normally, by now, she would have caught herself and stared at her bleeding knuckles in disbelief, in true shock that she held this sort of anger inside of her, that she was capable of destroying the world around her if only she let herself, but no. She kept punching. She kept slamming her hand into the mirror. She kept screaming. She kept crying. She kept bleeding. She couldn't stop herself now. She was too far gone; she didn't know how to.

Crossing the point of no return was foreign to her. She didn't know exactly what it would feel like when she would, and she didn't quite remember what had happened to lead to it. She could barely even remember a time before that, not in a state like this. Any thought that may have interrupted her blind, unchecked rage was to be dismissed and sent to the back of her mind, to be ignored until they piled up and finally reigned her in.

Punch. And then another. They kept coming. She didn't know what to do. She didn't know what else there *was* to do. She couldn't do anything, could she? She was powerless. Violet was powerless. Penelope was dead. There was nothing she could do about it, and there was nothing she knew about it besides that horrific fact that tortured her mind.

She couldn't do anything. She would smile, and wave, and say 'I'm fine,' as she always had, and deep inside she would breed a hatred – an unconstrained, rabid choler that festered inside her like a disease waiting to claim a victim, and still wouldn't be able to do anything.

No number of words, or phrases, or sentences, or paragraphs, or pages, or novels, or libraries could ever describe what she felt like. It was difficult for her to even conceive the thought that she was actually doing what she was doing, that she was punching and punching and punching relentlessly at this mirror to pound it into nothing but a fine, dangerous dust, one that she would hold back the urge to breathe in and die from, just to torture herself more–

Punch. And again. And once more. And she would keep punching. For a moment, she would see the reflection of her mother, and punch harder. And for a moment, she would see the reflection of her father, and punch even harder. And for a moment, she would see the reflection of her brother, and punch so hard that she swore she had broken every bone in her clenched fist, and she would keep punching regardless. She didn't care. She didn't care about anything anymore. She just wanted to punch. She wanted to destroy. She wanted to get this visceral, all-consuming rage out, once and for all.

Violet knew inside, maybe subconsciously, that she needed to exhume these feelings. She couldn't just bury and burn them away, or pretend they would simply leave her, knowing too well, all too well, that they would only circle her mind like a siren, to hypnotise her into a state of true insanity. She had to get it out of her. She couldn't take it anymore. She couldn't bear it. She would keep punching and punching and punching, because what else was she supposed to do?

She had to destroy it. She had to get rid of it. She had to get rid of these feelings. They were unladylike. They were unbefitting of a woman like her. Of a *lady* like her. She had to destroy it all. She needed to. She craved it. She craved the destruction, the thoroughgoing rage that would destroy anything in its wake, that would set a fire alight inside her that spread to anything she saw fit to watch burn and wither away, like all her passions and desires the moment she learned that these feelings were shameful.

Did feeling like this make her shameful? Did her irrational, erratic behaviour make her shameful? Did her lack of skill in dealing with these problems and emotions make her shameful? Or was it the emotion itself, the emotion of anger, *real* anger, that carried the shame itself, and tainted anybody who felt even the slightest, delicate brush of its power?

What exactly about anger was so shameful?

Why had she been taught that this was shameful?

Was everyone who believed that anger is shameful right?

Questions to answer later. Now, she needed to focus. She needed to punch. She needed to destroy. She needed to erase.

But, for a moment, she stopped.

She stopped punching.

She stopped punching, and turned her hand over, to ogle the sanguine liquid littering each crack and crevice of her hand. She stared into the red, and how it wept from each cut in her porcelain skin, to dribble down her fingers and coat her nails in a thin, translucent red, then dripping onto the cracks of the mirror. She watched as her hand, once white in colour, became stained and sullied with a bright, sombre red, and thought.

She sat back on her legs. She sat back and thought. She ignored the glass cutting into her stockings, tearing through to reach out to the skin of her knees, ripping through that too. She ignored the reflection of her blank face in the remaining bits of mirror beneath her, simply to think to herself for a moment. She wasn't thinking about the consequences of her actions, or buying a new mirror, or the blood extorting itself from her body, or the tears rolling out of her face in their millions.

On some level, she wasn't even thinking all that much. Maybe an occasional thought would cross her mind, but it all sounded like garbled nonsense to her dead state of being, as if her mind was slowly powering down from the energy she had unearthed, and the power over the mirror she had exercised. Perhaps, she would think of bandages, and how she would need to do something or other with them – at the time, she was rather high on adrenaline and also quite unaware of her current state – or maybe how she felt a little light-headed and considerably tired.

To give her the benefit of the doubt, she was doing her best to understand. She didn't know what she was doing, or why she was doing it; at the time, at least; but she knew she had done something. God knows what she had done, but she had done it. She had punched a mirror. She had punched her reflection. Had she punched herself? Had she punched the glass? Had she punched what she saw in the mirror in an inexplicable rage, or had she punched the mirror for the sake of disentombing such a rage?

She didn't know. She didn't know all that much about her feelings, in reality, despite her academic knowledge. A smart woman, Violet was; being a doctor in medicine and theoretical science was definitely no easy feat, for a woman of her time and age, no less than any individual who had chosen to pursue such a career path. The point was, despite her intelligence, she had no clue how to deal with this. She had learned how to dissect a human being, but not how to dissect her traumatic experiences. She had learned how to understand quantum uncertainty, but not how to understand her own feelings and the world around her.

Was this how things were meant to be? Was this the fate she was destined for? Was this a fault of her younger self, for making the decision to stray from her parents, or was this some sort of unknown power at work? Was she supposed to be angry? Upset? Happy? Disgusted? Emotionless? Was she meant to preserve true stoicism in the fear that, God forbid, she shows an ounce of emotion, or was she meant to break mirrors and windows and let her hands bleed and let her legs ache and let her tears fall and be truly, comprehensively angry?

She couldn't produce an answer to that. All she could do was kneel there, analysing the cuts in her hand blankly. She would extend her fingers, and it would hurt more. It almost felt therapeutic, the way the glass dug into her hands and *reminded her of her own humanity.*

She was still human. She was a human being. She was a real human being, made of flesh and blood and emotions and aspirations and dreams and desires and hatred and anger and rage and disappointment and all the things she had and all of the things she lacked. There were a *lot* of things she lacked, both now and in her past.

And it all made sense.

Standing to her feet, hands shaking from all manners of agonizing pains, fear of her own strength and power, confusion as to why she was doing anything and simply an inordinate amount of loss of her identity, she stumbled backwards with her eyes fixated on that *damn mirror* while her mind raced and her feet stepped and her heart beat and her hands shook and everything seemed to happen at once and all she could do was watch. She could just watch. She could watch, she had to watch, as everything she knew fell apart, as the ground crumbled beneath her, and she was left to fall through the abyss of nothing.

It threatened to swallow her whole, to grip onto her ankles and inch its way up every square centimetre of skin, to claw at her and tear her flesh straight from its bone and drag her unceremoniously into its chokehold, to strangle her and silence her and remind her of why exactly these sorts of outbursts were so shameful. The shards of mirror that had landed around her stared her down, judging her every move as the pupils of her eyes constricted to meet her own.

This wasn't about the mirror anymore.

Interlude III.

A Brief Moment of Realisation

"I remember her father. Wherever he would go, she would follow along; like a chick to its mother hen, if the mother hen ruled by lashing the chick into line every time it took a step outside of the line of its brethren."

He walked. She followed.

"Violet."

"Yes, father?"

"Your brother and I have been talking." His voice was stern as ever; unmoving, yet intelligent to the inner workings of her mind. He knew what hurt.

"About what—?"

"You speak when you are *spoken to*." He cut her off harshly. A warning left his lips, and Violet shut her own promptly, nodding to herself in shame. She, too, knew what hurt. She knew that he knew what hurt. A momentary silence encompassed the stoic individuals – Violet's persistent stoicism had always branched from her father's own – before her father called to her once more. "Speak."

"About what have you been speaking, father?" Her gentle, never-wavering tone came once more, speaking calmly. In truth, she was fearful of him; greatly so; but refused to allow any sign of despair or grief show from within her body. It beat on the cage of her heart, gripping at each rib and threatening to just about peek out, but she kept it down. God knew what would happen if she ever showed the incorrect emotion around him, and so did she. She knew, all too well.

However, Violet refused to ever acknowledge any of the transgressions against her. To her, this was just how things were meant to be. Perhaps, one day, she would successfully escape it all, to be free to express herself and be her own person, no longer bound by the curling vines and sharp thorns prying into her fingers and palms. For now, she stayed, prisoner to her father's wrath and her mother's manipulation. She couldn't help but wonder if such a fate was everlasting for her, and she severely hoped it wasn't.

Her train of thought was quickly interrupted by none other than her father. "About you," he began, continually striding through the hallways, littered with all sorts of works of art, by many upperclassmen and the like, "and your life at school." Vincent – her father – took close note of her flinch, and how she tried to disguise it as brushing something from the skirt she wore, his eyes narrowing as the corners of his mouth turned upwards in disgust.

"Speak." He mumbled, in a clear disdain, ascertaining to his acknowledgement of her nervousness.

With an equipped deride, she spoke again. "What of my life at school?" She was so close to being found out. She couldn't. She *couldn't*. Who could have told him? Who would have known? Michael didn't go to her school. Perhaps, he could have found out, but she couldn't imagine how, in that very moment. That aside, the only other person who could have known didn't even *exist* to her parents (because only the Lord God would know what would happen, to not only her, but them, too).

"Stop trembling." And so, she stopped. "What do you make of our family, Violet?" He raised his eyebrows, appearing surprisingly intelligent as he stopped in front of a portrait. The mother of Violet's mother. She was, surprisingly, of Polish descent, as was her mother, as was Violet. Her father was of the French heritage her current family had leaned towards, potentially as Poland was a rather unstable country, and seemed to refuse to exist within the bounds of Earth quite commonly. Regardless, Violet possessed a certain fluency in Polish, as she did in French, as she did in English. A talented woman, pertaining to her age, gender and status. "Speak."

She spoke. "Our name is important to me. I find it to be rather beautiful, Father," she fought the smile begging to appear upon her lips back, "and I understand its importance, not only to me, but to the public, too." Concluding her momentary monologue, she left a soft sigh rolling from her lips, to fall upon the air in front of her. "Why do you as—"

"Speak when you are spoken to, you impudent brat!" He raised his gloved hand against her, to strike her left cheek, watching heartlessly as she tumbled to the floor in a pile of limbs, fabric and regrets, regrets that potentially weighed more than all the beautiful dress she wore combined with her body weight, not moving a muscle as she regained herself to stand to her feet shakily, a soft, red mark appearing upon the cheek he had slapped. She made no sound as she rebounded from his hit, a dainty hand settled upon her cheek to try and alleviate the pain as best she could. "Speak."

"Apologies, father," was all she could mumble out, biting back tears welling in her eyes and venom bubbling in her throat and her very own set of punches aching in her knuckles. Instead, she simply apologised to him, and moved on from the entire situation. After all, this wasn't out of the ordinary. If she wanted to make a big deal out of this, she shouldn't have tolerated the injustices from the start – though, to give her the benefit of the doubt, what was a seven-year-old to do, against her adult father, when he had the absolute authority to beat her to a pulp and cut her to ribbons and reduce her to a slab of meat, a commodity, a *thing*?

Despite her brewing anger, from the years of torture she had sustained, she waited for him to either speak once more, or to command her to do so. She waited. A minute went by. Maybe two, or perhaps even three, if she had counted the seconds correctly. Nothing. There were tears in her eyes, but she dared not cry them. Any sort of emotion after she had been hit was false. Apparently, it was a carefully calculated trap; something to weasel guilt out of her peers, for them to feel bad for her and pity her. She didn't need pity. She didn't need anybody to feel bad for her. She was fine. Nothing was wrong. So, she dared not cry the tears that would give away that something was.

"We think your school is having a negative, repercussive effect on you." Her father spoke, indifferently, autocratically, once more. "Your mother – of course, with her womanly *bathos* – disagrees. I'm sure you will too, seeing as you possess that exact same melodramatic characteristic." His hisses and sibilation of her human emotions only grew the seeds he had planted in his daughter's mind, the ones with 'disdain' and 'shame' spelled all over them; it was almost as if he was curating the well-tamed Land of Nod within her mind, biding his time until the roses bloomed and the thorns sank into her mind, and the wasps of ignorance and desperation threatened to sting her brain and begged to poison her mind, fertilising the soil for new seeds in a sickening cycle. "Speak."

"I don't understand what you mean," Violet asked, and her voice shook. She had already been hit once, expectant of a second beating, but nothing came of his reprise to her phrase. She looked up at him. He refused to look down at her. Even the round, hazel eyes that looked up at him with an unexplainable sorrow, with a despair not even the bounds of human language could describe, were not enough to convince him to spare her even the flicker of his attention. Too much, and the beautiful roses in her Land of Nod would wilt and rot into weeds.

Silence came about them once again. Neither dared to say anything, for their own individual reasons, and simply stood before their collective ancestor in silence. Violet's father had speechlessly allowed her to drift from his side, just a step or two, to analyse the portrait before her. Of course, Violet had vague memories of her grandmother – not an awful lot, but enough to have a rough idea of what she was like. She was a rather enigmatic woman, however; Violet could never tell exactly what she was thinking. Regardless, she stared at the portrait, with a certain curiosity for its majesty. She had seen it once or twice, in the same hallway, and read the golden plaque fixed to the wall beneath it many times before, as if some sort of consolation for the fact that she didn't have much of a relationship with the woman:

Rozalia Łatkowska

Mother to Noelle Łatkowska-LaFramboise

1899 - 1957

"I mean that you and your mother are both as… *utterly* emotional as each other." Her father started up again, after the lengthy pause between his last response to her forced inquiry – he would beat her if she spoke out of line, and if she didn't speak at all – then continued abruptly. "At some point, I would consider it detrimental." Stretching his arms out as he extended his berating, Violet had seemed to lose interest in his incessant bickering with nobody, though kept an ear open, in case she was provoked to respond. "I mean, honestly. How on Earth are you supposed to get things done, at this rate? You'd never survive without me."

For a moment, Violet's teeth sank into her tongue, biting the soft flesh but taking care to not pierce it within her mouth. If there was one thing that she hated, even more than her father, it was her father's constant degradation of women, as if he wasn't born from one and hadn't married one himself. At least me and your brother aren't as socially and internally inept as you and your mother. After all, you're a woman. It's in your nature to be… *pathetically* sentimental, all the time." He never thought back to his own mother, or his wife's mother, or their mothers before them, when he spoke so lowly of women. He imagined that their husbands, and their fathers, and their fathers before them, would all align themselves with him. After all, that was simply how things were, then and now.

That was just how things were meant to be.

Stage VII.

Depression

"After losing control, she… lost control. I don't really know how else to describe it. She went manic, I suppose, and then just… stopped. She stopped doing anything. I still can't figure out what her reasoning behind it was.
I still don't regret what I did."

"Just leave me be. I don't want company, nor do I need it."

"I am not leaving you here like this, Violet."

"Dr. Ludwig, I swear to God, I'm going to kill you. Get out of my house."

"That's fine. As long as you are safe. I'm not going to let you destroy yourself from the inside out."

"... I don't even have the energy to fight you on this."

She let out a heavy sigh after Friedrich concluded his point, sheathing herself beneath her bedsheets again, ignoring the other's comforting palm against her fabric-coated shoulder. "Why do you even care? After you sent my parents after me, I thought that was a declaration of war." Rolling her eyes, she folded her arms from beneath the blanket, still breathing shakily. She wasn't all too aware of what was going on and happening around her, but she still somewhat had the strength to argue.

"... I didn't know. Can we not bring this up?" He knew that begging for her forgiveness, or for her to just stop reminding him of how badly he had messed up, was futile, but tried anyway in the desolate hope he could scrape in his mind that maybe, just *maybe*, she would take pity on him and his wishes, instead of focusing on the sorrow and guilt of herself. It wasn't often that she tried to shirk the blame away from herself, especially so when it was the fault of someone she cared about, but there was no harm in trying, Friedrich supposed.

"Not bring what up?" She started, giving him a blank stare from over her shoulder, sleepy tears welled in her eyes and aching to sink into the pillow she laid on. She wasn't in the mood to argue, nor was she in the mood to forgive. "How badly you fucked up? Sure, I'll shut my mouth about it." Violet then flopped over onto the pillows again, nestling herself within the fluff and comfort of the blankets and duvets, still trying to ignore him as she hoped he would fight for her attention again.

Sighing as he pressed a palm to his face in disappointment – which is what he expected, but nonetheless didn't lessen the blow of her words one bit – he removed his other hand from her shoulder to place it neatly in his lap, still trying to remove himself from the drained knell of her patronising voice. "Listen, I didn't know it would end up like *that*. You never tell anyone about your parents – how was I supposed to know?"

"You could have started by not lying to me." She huffed after that, covering her head with the duvet, sinking her head into the pillow beneath her to ignore him more. She didn't want any company in the first place, seeing as she was nowhere near fit to be a host in a mental state like that, let alone the man who had worsened her spiral indirectly. Violet settled to ignore him, at least until he said something that would trigger another meltdown or outburst or whatever her falsely guilty conscience would come up with next. "That would be nice."

"I didn't expect things to go the way they did. I would have come, I swear, Violet."

"But you didn't."

"Things came up! I promise you, if I had the opportunity to go, I would."

"But you still didn't come, did you? I don't recall you being here. I recall my father, smacking me across the face, full force."

Things went silent after that. He couldn't refute what had happened, or accuse her of lying – the bruise mark, there on her right cheek, had exploded like a bomb, from a solitary red to a conquering purple and green, littering itself across the porcelain of her cheek, as if a discordant crack had been forced into the harmony of her face. Sitting upon the corner of her bed, he stood himself up, placing his hands firmly upon his knees to help himself right his posture.

"Fine. I'll go, then."

Before he could make another move toward the door, Violet sat up in her bed, tears filling her eyes, highlighting each crevice of green in the sea of hazel iris. "... What did you say?" The fear, the undeniable despair that just screamed pity and sorrow in her voice was simply palpable, and each crackle and break in her tone only furthered the idea that she was afraid of being alone again. She couldn't be trusted alone.

"I said, I'll go. If you don't want – or even need – company, I will leave you be." He took his tweed coat from the hanger beside her door, and the flat cap, too, situating it on his head before finding the desperate woman stood in front of him, hands kept close to her chest, passing over one another in anguish. "What? Are you okay?"

"Oh, please don't go. Please. I…" She trailed off after that but clutched onto the sleeve of his coat that he had managed to put on before noticing her. Again, being barely aware of what she was doing, she bowed her head to him, trying to keep her tears from his coat, allowing them to fall to the floor as she sank to her knees, clinging to his boot in nothing but true desperation. He only took out his pocket watch to check the time.

"Why should I stay? You clearly don't need anybody around you, you said it yourself. You seemed perfectly content with rotting away in your bed, alone, aren't you? To wither away and die from starvation, or dehydration, or something along those lines." He crouched down, not long after that, and stared her right in those pitiful pair of eyes, eyebrows raised in insouciance, fixing his flat cap promptly as he stared her down, never daring to follow each tear ball that fell dramatically from her bottom eyelid, gliding through the air to re-join her cheek and fall to the floor. "So, tell me, Violet," he placed a hand underneath her chin, giving her his brawniest glance, "why should I stay with you?"

"I need you," she begged, scrambling for the cuff of his coat, gripping it tightly as she held onto him, now finding it easier to meet his eye in his crouched position. She curled up on his dress-shoes and cried dramatically, and begged him to stay, and let each tear fall to the wooden floor beneath her or roll from his shoe or sink into her nightgown or do anything to keep him there. She didn't care how shameful or embarrassing or disgraceful or unladylike it was. She was desperate, and she would do anything to have him stay. "I need you. I need you here with me. I don't care. Do what you want to me, do what you want with me, with my house, take what you need, take what you want. I can't do this anymore. I can't be alone anymore."

At first, Friedrich felt the urge to make a sarcastic remark, but then stopped himself. His unhinged jaw shut, and he dared not comment further for the moment that he let the realisation hit him. "You don't trust yourself alone, do you?" Mumbling out the sentence with a slight waver in his tone, Friedrich lifted himself up, with her in his arms, to seat her on the bed as she clung to him desperately. He hadn't realised her actions before, her defensiveness merely being a façade for her insecurity and fear of her own self, that she only wanted nothing more than for him to stay.

"Wait here, I'll make you some tea, okay?" Standing to his feet and trying to steady himself as quickly as he could, he made haste in moving past her doorway to enter the hallway outside of her room. The wallpapers had gathered a substantial amount of dust, and the paintings in the picture frames of angels and flower fields and heavenly scenes were tainted with the weathering of age and time. Even the doorknobs, once preened and shined to the point that one's face could be seen within the reflection, was clouded beyond recognition, as if it was designed to look sad and poorly.

Making his way down the creaking stairwell, he took note of the tattered home, how the spiders nestled themselves into the corners and crevices of each wall, how the windows fogged and clouded not with the condensation of the outside world but of dust and debris from weeks of Violet's internal refusal to clean, and how the carpets on the bottom floor had faded into a grey, desaturated version of their once lively and bright colours. The wall to his left had two holes poked into the dirtied cream wallpaper, and the shelf that once rested upon the wall had fallen to the floor.

The belongings of such a shelf had scattered themselves out on the floor individually, as if to perfectly separate themselves from one another. A candle, with a glass casing around the wax that had shattered, leaving the ball of what once could have been considered a candle rolled a pace or two away from the shattered specks and flecks of glass about the carpet, nestled into the locks of dust-drenched fluff. Then, beside that candle, a pile of books — something or other about theoretical, quantum or experimental physics — that had splayed themselves out surprisingly neatly, compared to the cacophony of the fallen candle.

Lastly, a small music box. This, Friedrich took a greater interest in. Picking it from the floor and blowing some of the dust off, sputtering and coughing away what little particles had managed to float their way into his throat, he took the small handle into his index finger and thumb and began to wind the music box in curiosity for what it would play.

The melody was slightly out of tune, considering the rust having grown on the music box with time, and it seemed to lag behind or become stuck at certain points where more than one note was being played, but the song it played was sweet and calm and almost triumphant, like it would conquer any evil and fell any villain, and maybe even instil a sense of unbreakable hope and determination in whoever listened to it. Friedrich, having been more than stressed out over her situation, definitely found some consolation in its solitary and yet uniting tune, placing it back in its original spot and even going so far as to make it look like he hadn't listened in to its melodic whispers and hums at all.

Making his way over to the kitchen with a little more life in him, he spent a moment searching for a mug within her five-or-so cupboards, turning the kettle on and leaning his back to the wall in anticipation. After a minute of waiting in dead silence, he pressed his hand to the side of the kettle to see that there was not even a heating sensation within the tips of his fingers, let alone the burn he had anticipated. Moving the kettle out of the way to try and investigate why nothing had happened, he noticed the plug of the kettle had been rightly jammed into the outlet, of which was switched off.

Mumbling some frustrated curse or other under his breath, Friedrich then flicked the kettle on and then proceeded to wait once more. Now, when he pressed his finger gently to the kettle's side, he found himself leaping back in a satisfying sort of agony, shaking off the burn on his fingertip with a more pleased than pained expression. At least the kettle was working. As it boiled, he leaned over to the rack of teabags she kept, taking a teabag within the section neatly labelled 'Earl Grey', placing it within the mug he had selected and fetching some milk from the fridge.

The whistle of the kettle was enough to startle him, and to have him return to the scene of his intricate tea-making. Pouring the water over the teabag, he then reached for a spoon within her drawer, stirring the sack of tea leaves engulfed by water cautiously, making sure not to burn himself again as he removed the bag with the string attached. Moving over to her bin, he threw away the teabag, and continued the process of curating her perfect tea. Having been roommates for their entire college life, Friedrich knew exactly how Violet liked her tea, and that she trusted him enough to make it for her, but it had been eight or so years since he had made tea like this.

Realising that Earl Grey tea didn't call for milk was one of his last feats, clicking his tongue and sighing as he placed the glass bottle back into the fridge and carefully took the mug by the handle to carry it upstairs. With every step he took upwards, he only realised more how long it had been since Violet had properly seen another person — excluding her brother from the equation, of course — and how badly she wanted, or, rather, needed, to interact with somebody outside of her family.

He took the tea back to Violet and offered it to her silently. She drank it, encased in that same, familiar silence, and they shared the silence in a moment of solidarity. Violet thanked him afterwards, then put the empty cup on the cabinet beside her, and they settled in the quiet, tranquil air around them.

Finally, a moment of peace.

Stage VIII.

Loneliness

"She withdrew from everything after a while. She just stopped interacting with people. Perhaps she was tired of explaining why I was gone to so many people who knew just about as much as she did."

She felt the urge to vomit as she stood in the doorway, watching the car pull away, tears streaming down her rosy cheeks and threatening to freeze up into little icicles on her perfect face as Friedrich drove further and further, ripping away his comforting presence along with each turn of the tires.

For a moment, every thought in her mind became organised. Stood in formation, rows and rows of vigilant soldiers in her brain, everything seemed to quell for a minute, or perhaps two, and she enjoyed this momentary silence as she closed the door to her cottage house and stepped inside. However, the silence became too much to bear at one point, in such an instantaneous manner, and she stopped in the hallway to try and come up with something to bring an unprecedented interest into her life again.

Friedrich wasn't going to stay forever. I thought we knew this well enough.

Yes, but that doesn't mean we couldn't hope for him to stay.

Just like we can hope for them to suddenly rise from the dead. I ask you; what is the point in doing any of that?

What is wrong with you? These two situations are nothing alike. He hasn't died, for God's sake.

But he could. You know how quickly Penelope passed away. Who's to say he won't crash the car he's driving right now and cause a horrific death unbefitting of someone who took the time out of their day to help someone as destitute and poor as you?

Let me guess. This is my fault because if I had never called him and involved him, he would have never driven here and subsequently crashed.

Only if you want it to be.

Why would I ever want that? You want that.

I don't. I'm simply telling you the truth of the matter. I see no fault in my logic — do you?

... No. No, I don't. But just because a chain of events led to this doesn't mean I in turn caused the crash. God– he

hasn't even crashed! Why are you painting these scenarios as if they are true?

I never said they were true. I said they were a possibility and if they <u>were</u> indeed true, you would be at fault.

No, I wouldn't. How could I have been the only one at fault for something completely out of my control?

Now look who's putting words in who's mouth. You fail to realise that you are coming to these horrible, blame-inducing conclusions yourself. All I have to do is merely prompt you, and you have the unbelievably spectacular talent of twisting this all to make yourself look like the victim.

I never said I was the victim. Why do you immediately amass me to be such a bad person?

Why is this behaviour considered 'bad'? I never considered this 'bad' behaviour. You are simply… Ill. Ill in the mind, is what you are.

Settling herself on the couch to stare lifelessly out of the window, watching each snow particle as it landed itself inconspicuously onto her window, only to melt away at the increased heat of the glass and form a small drop of water on its surface, Violet gripped onto the remote and moved to turn the television on, but frowned at the lack of noise. Finally breaking her locked stare at the window, she realised quickly that she was trying to turn on a TV that she had shattered weeks ago, and rolled her eyes at her rather embarrassing blunder, curling up on her couch and throwing a pillow over her head to try and ignore the bickering in her mind.

After all, it wasn't like she could help these sorts of thoughts. Perhaps, one day, they would be more violent and destructive than other days, and the lack of formation of conscious, rational thought would send those neat, orderly soldiers within her mind into a mayhem of friendly-fire, guns blazing, blood splattering, voices screaming for any sort of cessation of the panic and horror of her thoughts, or they would be collected and imitate a sense of rationality and sanity, when in actuality the squadron leader was detailing how each and every stray thought she conceived would get the equivalent of a crucifixion's worth of ridicule and shaming, and they would stand to attention and follow such orders promptly. Anybody who stepped out of line would be shot dead in an instant, after being made a fool of in her mind.

Now, this was not to say Violet was insane; the border between her slipping compassionate morality and the unhinged nature of the thoughts she was nanoseconds away from acting on became thinner and scarcer with every day that passed by, but for the most part she retained just enough a stable level of control in her life to not descend into a state of absolute psychopathy. She had found herself feeling less empathetic for people around her, and focused more on the negativity and qualms of her own life, wanting to take it out on anyone — or anything — that stood in the way of the wake she created, one that would consume and tear apart anything that made a pathetic attempt to oppose it, but didn't dare speak of such desires, let alone act on them as often as the squadron leader of her mind told her to, lest she be admitted to a mental hospital. The last thing she wanted was to lose her mind, at this stage of her life.

Do you really think for one moment that we are ill in the mind?

Of course, I do. Just two days ago, Friedrich was injured at the cause of our outbursts, and <u>we didn't even apologise</u>. That's the worst of it. We didn't even care. <u>I</u> didn't even care. I could have urged you to at the very least mention it to him and ask him for forgiveness, but I left it because I simply <u>didn't care</u>. Do you know how sick you must be in the head to think like that? There is something seriously wrong with us, and one of us clearly knows it better than the other.

What do you want to do about it? Admit us to a psychiatric ward? Go back and apologise after two days of acting like nothing happened? God forbid, do you want to tell Mother and Father? Because whatever you're suggesting sounds an awful lot like a strangely worded death wish.

Perhaps it is. Perhaps, that is the only thing that will liberate us from this seemingly never-ending suffering.

Are you suggesting we commit suicide? After everything we've worked for. What about your family? Friedrich? Living for Penelope, experiencing all the things they didn't have the opportunity to? Why would that ever cross your mind as a viable option in this situation? You truly <u>are</u> sick in the mind.

Do you really want to live like this anymore?

It won't last forever.

With the way things have happened, you don't know that for sure.

Things will get better. Friedrich came to see us, to make sure we were doing okay; was that not better than being alone with <u>you</u> all of the time?

I suppose so, but was it better for him? You're right, in the most selfish manner possible, that yes, this was better for us, but not for him. We did hurt him, don't forget. How could that possibly be beneficial for him?

Because he wanted to come and see us. He <u>owed</u> it to us.

He didn't owe you shit, you entitled idiot! Your problems are exactly that: <u>yours</u>. Stop feeling sorry for yourself. You are genuinely, truly pathetic.

... I know.

Having curled herself up on the couch, Violet stared off into the distance of her home, unable to conjure up any sort of cohesive thought that would shut out and silence the constant bickering of her thoughts. She wanted to mumble something out, just to break the incessant quiet of her strangling house, gasping for air through tears as the oxygen around her formed itself into a hand, holding a tight-fisted grip onto her throat and clamping down on every square centimetre of skin it could get its liberating, freeing hand across, grabbing hold and threatening to never let go. Her soft whimper had dissipated such a hand away, unshackling her from its iron clutch, causing her to trace a hand against the non-existent wounds of her suffering along her throat.

She felt the barb-like thorns across her hand scratch into her porcelain skin, crackling and shattering the perfection of her neck and chest, coating it in scrapes of the beautifully destructive, red roses against her skin. Each perfect petal gilded with a carnal, blood red drifted against her skin delicately, with the same angelic delicacy that her skin portrayed itself, almost to mock and make a mimicry of her entire being whilst tearing into the fabric of something so undeniably perfect. The roses were a sense of false hope, as if to promise beauty and salvation and some semblance of a release from the nightmare she had been unwittingly planted into but dug into her at every given moment and only tied her to the ground they had been seeded in more. Every step of progress she tried to make would be countered, with more vines laced with thorns curling around her ankles and wrists, making even the conception of the thought of movement painful to merely think about.

Living like this was difficult. Naturally — she couldn't bear to stay in the position she was in any longer, because every moment she stayed the exact same way, the toxins of the rose would force themselves deeper into her arms and legs, into her torso and cranium, to drive themselves to her very core and implant them into her body relentlessly. Violet did want to free herself from these inhibitions and restrains desperately, to break away from the restrictions she was burdened with and grow from the experiences she had been sent through against her will, but, yet again, found every step of the path to recovery agonisingly tiring and, once all was said and done, the vines would drag her further backwards to where she had started. Now, she could only look on, miles away from where she had started.

Perhaps, things were not going to improve as she hoped they would.

Interlude IV.

A Divergence in Life

"Will there ever be a place in Heaven for the misguided from the light? Will she join me? I don't know, I couldn't tell you. I hoped desperately for her to find a way to change, and I think at some point she did too, but it never seemed to work out for her. She never valued herself or thought she would amount to anything, and neither did her peers. I did, but they didn't.
... At least, somebody else did. One other person. I don't think she would have survived without him."

"So, Violet," the therapist began, hands folded in her lap as she onlooked the trembling woman on the plush couch in front of her, "how do you view yourself? Positively? Negatively? Feel free to speak your mind here."

"You can tell me what to think and do and where to go, but I doubt that I would ever truly internalize the positivity you try and spread." Feeling an urge to stand and take her leave, Violet made the conscious choice to stay put. Despite her confliction, she continued to argue her case as to why this was pointless in her naturally eloquent manner. "My heart won't ever change, even if you shatter it and mend it from scratch."

"So, you see yourself as this unchanging force? Somebody who won't move, no matter what anybody tells you?" Questioned the therapist, rather poignantly.

"Well, when you phrase it like that, then yes." Violet answered her waveringly but became firmer and more confident in her answer as her hands unintentionally tightened into fists. "Yes, I do."

The therapist then paused, perhaps to write something down relevant to her case in her notepad, then looked up again. "How about a general statement of your self-worth?"

"It's non-existent, in all honesty."

"So, you have no self-worth? You don't hold value to anybody in your life at all? I don't know if it's my place to say, but I find that hard to believe."

"I don't believe it is your place to say."

"Then I apologise. Do you forgive me?"

"Sure?" Violet couldn't help but sew in a questioning tone to her statement, confused as to why she was even asking in the first place. She didn't care either way whether the therapist disrespected her or not; she had experienced enough transgressions to tolerate something as stupid as forgiveness for a slip of the tongue. "In regard to your previous query, I find it quite plausible that I don't amount to anything. My parents constantly abused me, as did my brother, and I faced numerous counts of assault and reckless behaviour simply for my identity and ethnicity throughout my school life. Consequently, I don't think people care all that much about me, similarly to how I don't care about myself."

"May I ask how old you are, Violet?"

"Twenty-three."

The therapist paused to write something again, in her notepad. Violet waited patiently and listened in attentively to her talking after she finished, now somewhat intrigued into what the supposed professional was spouting. "So, your lack of belief in your own value stems from the fact that you were mistreated as a child and young adult?"

"Sort of."

"Elaborate, please?"

Taking a deep breath and sighing it out, giving the therapist a blank stare as if to scream 'do I have to?' in her face, Violet began to speak once again. After all, who cared about what she knew? All this session was confidential, and a meagre therapist had no right to contact the authorities anyway. "I don't only believe I'm worthless because of the people around me. That's just ridiculous and foolish. I haven't contributed anything at all to society in the recent years, and I don't believe I'll amount to much in whatever future is left for me. My mind refuses to heal when I try to get better, and almost… *craves* being bad, like it's the only thing I know. How pathetic is that, right?" Violet tried to laugh at her own expense, but the therapist only gave her a pensive, unamused glance in response.

"Violet, do you mind me asking if you have any qualifications?"

"Master's degree in engineering from MIT, doctorate in both theoretical science from CalTech and independent medicine studies – recognised by the GMC, mind you – and a master's in surgery, also recognised." She listed off her impressive amount of education, counting it off on her hands and gesturing a little as she leaned back into the cushions of the couch. "But what does any of that matter? I did all those degrees and whatever when I still had a reason to be alive. I've expended my usage on Earth, and now I have no use or purpose."

"Violet," the therapist began, a more concerned glance on her face as she spoke, clicking her pen back and forth to an open and closed configuration, tapping it against her page delicately and on occasion, "how often does this cross your mind? Do you think about your place in the universe often?

Do you think you don't belong in it, or something along these lines?"

"What does it matter?" She shrugged nonchalantly to the other's query, leaning back in an ordinary fashion. She found an unladylike position, unbefitting of her to keep herself in, to settle into, and continued to argue back and forth with the woman trying to provide her consolation. For somebody who had walked in willingly, trying to help herself, she was putting up quite the fight to oppose her. "Everyone has these sorts of thoughts sometimes, where they feel they don't have a purpose to be alive on Earth. Everyone will eventually find themselves in a place where they don't belong, and–"

"That isn't entirely true." Violet's attention had been caught almost immediately as the therapist cut through her words instantly. Obviously, she wasn't entirely sure as to what the therapist was getting at but decided to give her undivided attention to the individual, leaned forward just slightly as she listened in to the horrors of the words that would drill themselves into her eardrums, like jackhammers pressing down on the stretched-out skin to force her to hear the woman out. "I won't say you are the only one struggling with these thoughts, because the fact of the matter is that you aren't. There are many people who, like you say, have trouble seeing their purpose in the universe and will often spiral and fall into rabbit holes trying to pursue things that they don't necessarily enjoy."

Violet raised a finger to interject, her jaw still open to try and contribute, but she was stopped by the therapist raising her hand authoritatively. "However," she answered Violet's non-verbal query sharply, and effectively shut her up for the moment that she wanted to continue speaking, "I think you will find it rather uncommon for people to have a constant stream of thoughts regarding their own existence in a negative light. Of course, when you look in certain demographics, these sorts of existential crises become more commonplace, but in somebody of your age group? Many of those your age are fully aware of their potential to make a name and meaningful life for themselves, and don't want to give up just yet."

A beat of tense silence.

"So, what about those who commit suicide?" Violet finally found the opportunity to speak, already stewing with rage after having been talked over by somebody who only knew such a surface-level understanding of her thoughts.

"What about them?"

"They can present as these average people that you speak of, those that don't even consider it at first – or lie on these trials and exams, of course – but are so good at concealing all of their negative emotions considering their self-worth, even from those who they may have confided in for years, only to suddenly disappear. Perhaps they'll leave a note behind, apologising for their transgressions against the world, or blaming people who never knew that had committed any wrongdoing against the individual committing suicide, but for the most part, people would never know that these people were ever suicidal. If somebody was unaware of the cause of death, it wouldn't even cross their mind as a possibility."

"And what of it? These sorts of cases are uncommon. There is most likely remnants of these individual's memoirs, diaries, letters or family relations that become telling as to why people commit suicide. Of course, it's complicated, because the psychology of an individual person, with all of their life experiences and connections taken into account, becomes rather complicated once all factors are considered. However, I won't negate your point; you are right in saying that sometimes people do… 'randomly' commit suicide. They manage to keep it under the radar for so long that nobody realises what has hit them when it happens." Another brief pause of silence, before the therapist finally met eyes with Violet. Neither of them dared to speak through the vulnerability, but the therapist was first to break such a thickened, clinging atmosphere. "Do you ever feel this way,

Violet? That people would or would not consider the fact you may commit suicide?"

"I've never been able to decipher what people think of me, in all honesty. Discovering that people have adverse or favourable opinions of me is almost epiphanous, in a sense, because it takes me far longer than the average person to finally find out that somebody may be in love with me, or stalking me, or wants to kill me, or wants to kiss me, or whatever they see fit to do with me." She answered calmly, comfortable with discussing such topics, leaning her head against the wall behind her in apathy as the therapist continued to question her promptly.

"And have you been in all of these scenarios before? Do you speak from experience?"

"I do." Then, another moment of silence. Neither seemed to want to provoke nor set the other off on another tangent, as if they were both stood on the bounds of a tightrope frozen in ice; one wrong move, and they would both be placed in a delicate balancing act for each other's trust to be won over again. "May I ask you a question?"

"Why?" The therapist looked up from her notepad, eyes thin and piercing.

"Why shouldn't I?" Violet's eyebrows furrowed at that, raising sceptically to mimic her own tonality at the therapist's challenging voice. What was the problem with her asking a question? Was she not here to discuss her issues? Perhaps this issue was too metaphorical for her to discuss. "Fine," she gave in, and subsequently silenced herself, "never mind."

"If you say so," the therapist commented loosely, and wrote down another few sentences upon her notepad's fresh page, flicking over as the sound of swishing paper sliced through the calm silence once again. She seemed so nonchalant and calm in everything that she did, in a way that almost seemed psychopathically collected, which definitely didn't help put Violet at any sort of ease. Regardless, she continued to discuss with the individual in the private room, ignorant of her own safety. "So, tell me: do you have any close friends? Any confidants, people you can trust, or are at the very least comfortable for you to talk to?"

"One. Perhaps two." Responded Violet, on command, as was the status quo for such a meeting. She was doing well with complying with the expectations and such.

"And may I know their names?"

"Penelope, and... Dr. Friedrich. Last names aren't important." Seeing the therapist open her mouth, Violet's cutthroat glare was enough to have her simply write down the names she had been given.

"And how do you feel about these people in relation to your own self-worth? Would you scale them as more worthy than you, or on the same level, or perhaps even less than such?"

"I would probably put them higher than myself. If I were to sacrifice them or myself, I would sacrifice myself before I even considered sacrificing them."

"But would you not consider an alternative to sacrifice?"

"No. I don't see a point in that."

"And why is that?" The therapist clicked her pen open, ready to write.

"Because this would finally be an end to my suffering, would it not? Haven't we just spent the past forty-five minutes discussing why exactly my life means nothing to people? About my family's torment and attacks against me, and how this escalated until I finally escaped? God, at this point I just *ache* to die! I don't even care how anymore!" Violet had now stood up, taking the coffee table before her within her hands as her wide, crazed eyes darted from every feature on the therapists face, back and forth frantically as she ranted. "I want someone to kill me! I want to kill myself! I want to die from natural causes, and I want to die from an unprecedented tragedy! Oh my God, I just want to *die!* There's nothing left for me here! What am I supposed to do anymore?!"

Her heaving breaths were the only thing that filled the silence as she continued her deranged, unwilling raving about her life problems and suicidal thoughts, pacing the room intensely as the therapist looked back and forth, still writing hastily as she spoke. "I don't serve any purpose to anybody, and I don't even like being alive! I take no pleasure or enjoyment in living my life like this! I have my degrees, and I have my home, and I like my job but *what does it all mean?* Who the fuck *cares* about any of this?! I don't even know who I am, God damn it! I can barely even remember what I'm doing here, why am I even talking to you?! What the Hell are you supposed to do about my fucked-up situation? You're just some shitty mall therapist I booked because I was feeling *too* sorry for myself."

Taking her coat from the hat-rack and slinging it over her shoulder, Violet murmured out a momentary "good day to you" and took her leave, slamming the door shut on her way out.

Why had she come there again? She didn't need help. She was normal, like the rest of them. Violet was just a normal woman with normal thoughts. There was nothing quite out of the ordinary or necessarily peculiar about her. She wasn't anomalous; of course not! That therapist was utterly ridiculous, if she felt the need to say so herself. All of this talk about not believing in Violet's story, and even having the nerve, the absolute cheek, to challenge her. How dare she. How was Violet supposed to get better if all she was faced with was opposition?

*

"What was she playing me for? *A fool?*" Violet had begun rambling to herself as she marched on home, barging past anybody who had the gall to get in the way of her predetermined path, glaring at anybody who decided to mumble some disdainful comment at her, shutting them up just as the therapist had shut her up. "I mean, *seriously,* she had the impudence to doubt me. I paid her to doubt me. I can't fucking believe this!" Throwing her arms up in the air a little, she noticed herself standing in front of a young man, perhaps her age or a few years older, looking at her with mildly fearful eyes for her state of being. "What? What could you *possibly* want that–"

"Your lips," he mumbled out, in a strong German accent, stumbling closer to her to peer further into her face. Naturally, Violet leaned back in reflex, but kept her eyes wide and on guard, watching his peculiar behaviour with a raised eyebrow. "They're blue. You must be freezing!" He quickly grasped a hold of her hand, and clasped his warm pair around it, watching as her shoulders sank and her expression began to soften ever so slightly. The heat in her face began to return, and the individual in front of her continued to warm her hand with his own. "How could you have thought to go out in cold weather like this, with no coat, nor a hat, not even a scarf to warm you? It's nearly November, and there's snow all around." He used one of his hands to adjust his rather thick glasses, peering up at Violet in perplexity. "Did you not realise?"

Violet then took a moment to lift her head. She looked around and felt the chill of the winter's breeze brush past her shoulders, inscribing a shiver into her body as she tightened her hand around the man who had stopped her needless rage. "No, I–..." She stopped herself, taking note of his genuine concern for an absolute stranger, her lips left parted in the momentary shock. He was absolutely right – the ground beneath her was littered with specks of snow, the same sorts of specks that fell upon her head and settled in the cracks beneath each ginger peal of hair, that had given her lips the purplish tint he had noticed before. "I didn't."

"Would you like to come with me, to my home? I can help you warm up, and perhaps perform a check-up on you, seeing as you seem to find it reasonable to go out in November weather like it's June." He commented loosely, stifling a laugh as he continued to try and warm her, removing his own thick, tweed coat to drape around her shoulders, aiding her arms into it. Seeing the fragile woman sink into the warmth of his jacket consoled his worries considerably, and he began to walk with her along the path, listening to her speak as they headed along together.

Violet had not much to articulate herself with, so simply nodded and began her line of questioning promptly. "Who are you? A local, perhaps? Or maybe a kidnapper preparing to lure me away and kill me?"

"If it puts your mind at ease, we can get to know each other. I'm merely looking out for another human's safety. Is that too difficult to believe?" He looked up at her – seeing as she was just a few inches taller – and continued to hold onto her hands, now removing his scarf to wrap around her own neck, smiling as she sank her chin into the fluffy fabric. "My name is Friedrich Ludwig. I am a local physician, maybe a town away, or so. Now, how about you?"

"... I'm Violet. Theoretical scientist. I... kind of live in the middle of nowhere."

"Well, it's nice to meet you, Miss Violet."

"... Nice to meet you too, Dr. Ludwig."

Stage IX.

Acceptance

"After a while, she moved on… In her own way, I suppose. Not in the sense that she would forget me; of course, she could never forget me. Maybe I <u>do</u> regret what I did. Just a little bit.
I didn't want her to get hurt, obviously."

"She's going to be okay. She's having respiratory problems and we strongly suspect she has asthma, so she'll stay in the hospital for a while, to make sure she recovers safely and gets the medication she needs. Do you know what happened to her?"

The doctor before Friedrich had questioned him calmly, a clipboard still in his hand, stood beside the hospital bed that Violet was settled in. She was sleeping peacefully, hooked up to a respirator, to make sure she was still getting the vital oxygen she needed to survive. Her skin was pale, unfeeling, almost as if she was already dead, despite the monitor beside her showing clearly that she was alive, but perhaps not well.

"I–… I do, vaguely…" He murmured out, uncertain of himself, shifting his weight from one foot to the other, barely aware of how to comprehend what he had witnessed mere hours ago.

"She was stood there, in the snow, unmoving," he began, clearing his throat, imagining what he had stumbled upon just to create a clearer image in his mind, "and she was murmuring something to herself. S– something about how she had waited for this day for so long, and how she would join 'them'. 'Them', of course, being her– um, her best friend, Penelope. She… she committed suicide a few weeks prior to this. Maybe a month or so, m– my memory is hazy."

The doctor continued to inscribe on the sheet in front of him, settling into a chair and pulling one over to allow the fellow doctor to do the same, noticing how his eyes widened as he recounted the event further, the fervour of his horror becoming more painfully obvious as he reviewed the situation in full. "Yes, she was stood there… I– I can recall it better now… Sh– she was shivering. She always had a taste for the cooler months," he couldn't help but laugh a little, pleased by the overtaking of the memory of their first encounter, and how he had given her his scarf and coat on that October day. He could remember it as clear as ever but didn't let himself dawdle on the information the other doctor wanted to know.

"I could see her tears; they were practically freezing on the skin of her face. She was shivering, and staring up at the sky, as if to look to God, yes, G– God himself, and ask 'please, take me up, because I am done here,' and I called her name, and she turned her head to see me. She was wearing barely anything, not quite naked, but maybe a short-sleeved top and a skirt, nothing like she would normally wear. Normally, she wears very thick, woollen clothing. But anyway, I– I digress," he ran a hand through his hair for a moment, still stressed over how she had stared at him, with those wide, pitiful, hazel eyes, and her hair blew in the wind like she had been carefully curated by the Heavens to look perfect even when she wasn't. He couldn't erase that image from his mind, the way she had turned her head so quickly to give him this look of desperation, the one that screamed 'please, help me' more than anything she could have said or done to him.

"She ran from me. And she wasn't a fast runner, but I was so perplexed by her... strange behaviour that it took me a long time to catch up to her. We were in the woods, by the way, so she found no trouble in running through the thick ploughs of snow around her, diverging through every trail and tree and shrub and just... I don't know what she was doing, but... I think she too was trying to commit suicide. And, I must admit, when I saw here stood there, staring up into the sky, it almost looked majestic. Almost. Like she was a sculpture of ice, with all of the snow building up on her head and shoulders, and the blizzard blowing around her with just– just no care for what she was doing, and her breaths were short and stifled but I would have quite liked to go out in the same way she did. It was poignant, in a grotesque, calloused sort of sense–"

"You're getting off topic, Dr. Ludwig." The doctor tapped his pen against his clipboard, and Friedrich adjusted his glasses promptly, clearing his throat as he nodded.

"Of course. M– my apologies, it's just… all rather confusing to think about. I– I mean, why? Well– I know why. You would too, if you knew the full extent… But yes, she ran away from me, and naturally, after regaining my bearings, I followed her, but it was so… surreal, to have everything just whizzing past me and my– my tunnel vision, it just focused on her and her billowing hair and the skirt she wore fraying behind her, and then she stopped for a moment. I nearly bumped into her, but I stopped too, and simply watched as she fell to her knees and hit the snow with a soft thud. I– I sprang into action, checking her vitals with whatever I had on hand, and pulling her into a clearing that had a little less snow. The colour, oh God, the colour in her face was *gone*, she was so… so pale, paler than normal, she has a very cool skin tone so she would normally be of a pink sort of hue naturally, but this was paper white, white like the snow around her, like the sun shining onto her face.

I feared that she would die. Truly, I didn't want that at all, and I mean– hey, I was doing my best to coat her in all sorts of blankets and coats and clothing I had on me – hence why I came into the hospital shirtless, and I– I express my gratitude for one of your shirts, but anyway – I did try my best to keep her warm, her pulse was so slow that I couldn't tell at all if she was alive. I picked her up, and now it was my turn to run, and only then I realised that she was so malnourished and underweight, and I knew she hadn't been taking care of herself. So, I realised, 'this is why her pulse is so– um, so slow' and 'this is why she fell over and couldn't run so fast' and 'this is why she's so thin' and, really, it hit me hardest knowing I was mostly at fault for this."

"Why is that, Dr. Ludwig? Have you any relation with this woman?" The doctor had finally looked up from his clipboard, pen pressed against the paper, as if preparing to mark something off.

"I… somewhat, yes, I do," he began, and noted the doctor ticking something off.

"Would you mind telling us what relation that might be, exactly?"

"... A friend." He hesitated, sparing her a forlorn glance, but continued regardless. "We've been friends for five or so years," swallowing heavily, he adjusted his glasses once again, making sure they sat properly on the bridge of his nose, just to occupy himself as he spoke, "and I was supposed to be aiding her recovery from the recent death of Penelope, the suicide I mentioned earlier. I called her parents first, because I got caught up with a lot of work at my local hospital, and I *promise* you, I really did intend to visit her and help her but I just *couldn't* at the time, and when I did go to visit she was just so… emotionally *and* physically cold, she was destitute and poorly and I did my best to help her but she would have terrifying outbursts at a constant, and I just… didn't know what to do, at some point."

Wiping away the tears that had gathered upon his lower eyelashes, the doctor continued to inscribe things into his page, flipping over to whatever he may have been hiding underneath to reference it constantly whilst he spoke. "I'm not going to prosecute you if you had any ill-intent against her. What matters is that you brought her here, and you're trying to help her now–"

"Why would you assume something like that about me?"

"You seem tense."

"I'm in love with her, you know. Romantically. I'm sure she doesn't feel the same way, but I do love her, dearly.

Ever since we met, I've felt connected to her. How could I have any ill-intent against somebody I care for so much?"

"Well," the doctor began, but thought better than to make a comment, and subsequently shut himself up. "Never mind. So, you've tried to help her constantly, but all of your efforts remained in vain? And what happened when you realised you couldn't help her?"

"I tried to leave, at some point. She told me she didn't need my help, but then when I told her I was going because she didn't need me – and, quite frankly, my patience had been run thin at that point – she begged me on her hands and knees to stay, clung to my leg and everything, and I pitied her so much that I did help her. The house was in a horrid, discordant state when I got there. It was like an atomic bomb had hit the home, and she simply took no notice of this because she never left her room. A shelf that was notorious for falling was indeed on the floor, with its contents all spread out from how it had fallen, and she had done nothing about it, and the dust that was all over the place was just… horrific to breathe in. Even her room was unpleasant to be in, so I did my best to clear up and keep to the kitchen for the most part.

I did most of her 'chores' for her; really, this just consisted of keeping her alive – or alive enough to be considered not quite dead yet – and making sure she had a healthy dose of human interaction with me to not go completely insane. And then, when I got enough calls from my hospital quite literally begging me to come into work, I told her that I genuinely had to leave and then she just… broke down. I didn't know how to feel, because, again, I pitied her a lot. Nobody, especially not her, deserved to feel so poor that they formed such an intense attachment to somebody, but I had to go. I couldn't do anything about it.

I did my best to try and ask for more time off, because it was so painfully clear that she needed it. I didn't want to take her to a mental hospital, because it would only reinforce her beliefs about her being 'crazy' or 'insane' for literally just *grieving* and I've heard that many hospitals nowadays are… questionable in their methods and practices of keeping people safe. Again, I digress, and I left."

A beat of silence came between the two doctors. "I… don't know what happened after that, in honesty. I just got a call from her yesterday, of her apologising for something or other, and that I would never have to be bothered by her again." He couldn't help but laugh at that, a solemn smile on his face as he turned his head to see her slumbering body, his heart skipping a beat every time he glanced at the heart monitor, and it showed any sort of potential of her life fading away. Of course, each anomaly would return to a natural, normal state, but he couldn't help but feel nervous each time it happened. "I would give my life to be 'bothered' by her, as she called it."

"Was she always this suicidal? Did she show signs of mental illness or deviation from the 'norm'?"

"From what I knew, mostly yes. She did have moments – and I cherish them dearly – where I could clearly peer into her soul and see that she was truly, genuinely happy, like when she was working on a new project or whenever we spent time away from our lives just to enjoy each other's company, but there were… many days that I was worried for her sanity. She would go on these crazed rants about her family and how much she hated them, and how she was justified in saying so because they hated her as much as she did, and perhaps even more. I didn't know what to think when she went on these sorts of rants, but… I must admit, they did scare me.

Not in the sense that I was afraid of her, because to be frank, I wasn't. I was afraid *for* her is a better way to describe it. She was rather sickly, and never paid much mind to her own health when she got caught up in these sorts of rants and incessant yells. I was typically the one picking her up after passing out on the couch, exhausted from anger, and pale in the face from barely stopping to take a life-saving breath. Don't even get me started on the mental repercussions of all this heated rage… Every day, she would wake up blankly, and one singular thing would set her off. It was literally like a– uh, how would you say it…?" He paused for a moment to think, then clicked his fingers in a pointed manner as he finally recalled the word that he wanted to use to describe what her short fuse was like. "A bomb–! Yes, like a bomb, ready to go off at any minute."

There was another second or two, or perhaps a minute, or maybe even two or potentially, it could have even been three of silence; it was hard to tell, seeing as the rigidity and solemnity of the situation was so high that it compared itself to some of mankind's tallest structures with grandeur and pride. Neither doctor spoke, one for a lack in line of questioning and other in regret and sorrow for what he could have done for the one he loved the most. "Did she often have these sorts of… outbursts?"

"Before? Not at all. She used to be so amicable and friendly, she was selectively mute for a time but… seemed to speak so fluently around me, like she trusted me with her voice and words and whatnot, but for the most part she was shy, and timid," he looked toward the bed which held Violet in its clutches, "and tender, and sweet, and lovely to be around…" Friedrich began to trail off, too busy admiring her to continue describing all of the positive thoughts he held about her, mumbling to himself with a lovestruck smile appearing on his face.

"–... Ludwig! Dr. Ludwig, please pay attention," the clicking from the doctor's hand quickly pulled him out of the trance he was settled into, blinking a little as he took the frame of his glasses in his hand and moved them about shakily on his face promptly.

"A– Apologies, doctor," he began, mumbling to himself a little as he let out a short, restrained laugh, looking up at him through his lenses as he let them go, "is there anything else you need from me?"

The doctor thoughts for a moment, taking the moment to adjust his own glasses, and then nodded to himself as he folded one leg over another. "No, I think you're free to go. Unless you'd like to stay by her side? I'm sure she'll be pleased to see you here, rather than a complete stranger. I doubt the feeling of abandonment would be helpful in a situation like hers." Noticing Friedrich's relieved laughter, he gave him an unimpressed glare, and stood up to leave, as did the man who had brought Violet there in the first place, moving to her side in haste.

"Violet?" He questioned softly, leaning down to near himself to her flitting eyelashes. "Are you awake?"

A soft hum was all she could let escape her mouth, raspy and disturbed, as she opened her eyes properly – well, as properly as she could, with the gas mask over her face and the extreme exhaustion washing over her body – to see him.

"Dr. Ludwig…?" She questioned, shakily, and reached her hand to smooth over his face, trying to feel out if it was him, on account of her poor sight.

"Please, my dear," he clasped a hand over her own, sighing in relief as she recognized him, "just call me Friedrich. With having known me for so long, I don't think there's a need for formalities anymore." He ran his thumb over the back of her hand and noticed how the colour in her face immediately began to draw, and the heart-rate monitor began to beep more and more as she refused to meet his eye.

"If you… um… say so." She forced out of her mouth, still breathing rather heavily, though obviously in a much better state than before, her chest heaving up and down less frantically as her heart began to calm. "Dr. Lu–... Freidrich," she corrected herself, finally choosing to make eye contact with him as she took the moment to pause and collect her thoughts. "May I ask you a question?"

Keeping her hand within his own, he pulled over the chair he was sitting in moments prior, settling into the slightly warm plastic with an extremely relieved smile upon his face. "You may," he laughed softly, allowing her to place her palm against his jaw again, embracing himself in the cold of her fingertips, ignoring the shiver it caused through his body. She was freezing, and he was willing to provide that warmth for her. Just as he had countless times before.

"Why did you come back for me? Why didn't you leave me?"

"How could I?"

A moment of hopeful silence.

"I treated you horribly. I'm sorry."

"You were grieving. I'm not going to be angry at you for feeling human emotions. I am very sure you didn't mean what you said, and I had practically already forgiven you the moment that I realised you cared for me so much."

"... What were you thinking about when you saw me, in the snow?"

"You. How worried I was for you, and how stupid I was to leave you."

"But what about your job–?"

Friedrich interrupted her promptly after that, clenching his own calloused, thick hand around her fragile, dainty, freckled own. "My job is nothing compared to what I would do for you. I would die if it meant you lived, Violet. I–... If I told you how much I cared about you, you wouldn't believe me, no matter how flowery or gruesome I made my description."

She let out a soft, muffled laugh after that, causing him to smile warmly at him. "Thank you... Friedrich." Violet finally widened her expression considerably, now a little more animate and able, to allow him to gaze into her hazel eyes with his own icy blue pair. "Did you think of anything else?"

"I... I hate to admit it, but I thought you looked beautiful."

Her eyebrows furrowed for a moment, and she settled upwards a little more, her back straightening against the plentiful of pillows behind her. "What do you mean?" She clearly wasn't offended by what he had said, rather, intrigued by what reasoning he may have had behind the comment.

"Well, you were stood there in the winter wind, with your hair flowing behind you, that drop of ginger in an ocean of white was... beautiful, in all honesty. And you were wearing all-white clothing too, all billowing in the wind, and you just... you looked so poignant and thought-provoked and for a moment I had the intrusive urge not to stop you. It was... maybe I shouldn't tell you–"

"No, please, do," Violet clasped both of her hands around his now, truly captivated by his talent to speak his mind, involved entirely in his honesty. "I'd... like to hear."

"Are you sure?" He questioned her readily, his face already heating from the way she had lurched forward to listen in more. Her nod prompted him to start once again, clearing his throat as he adjusted his spectacles, eliciting a laugh from her. "It was a horrid thought, really, to think that I would leave you there to die and watch as you froze over.

But you… you looked so exalted and struck by the beauty of the sky above you that it looked like a heart-rending painting, one that wrenched your heart of any emotions to leave a solemn bitterness and plaintiveness, like a black oil coating it, and… it was mesmerising to see. Like an exhibition of sorts." He shrugged a little, seeing how she nodded and leaned back again, tightening his grasp on her hand with an awkward smile, "perhaps I have confirmation bias. After all… I am rather enthralled with you, Violet. It's no secret that I'm in love with you."

She looked up, her eyes widened again. "Do you mean that? Or are you saying that to console me."

"Have I ever told you something I don't mean?"

"… Would you believe me if I told you I feel the same way?"

"Are you just saying that to console me or cushion my feelings?"

She paused. "No. I'm not. I really do love you; I promise."

"Well, I believe you when you say that. I trust that you wouldn't lie to me."

"I… I'm glad. And… I think I trust you too."

"Thank you, Violet."

"… You're welcome, Friedrich."